DEADLY WATER

BRENT TOWNS

WITH

SAM TOWNS

WOLFPACK
PUBLISHING
— EST 2013 —

Deadly Water

Paperback Edition
Copyright © 2020 Brent Towns, Sam Towns

Wolfpack Publishing
6032 Wheat Penny Avenue
Las Vegas, NV 89122

wolfpackpublishing.com

Paperback ISBN 978-1-64734-008-7
eBook ISBN 978-1-64734-007-0

DEADLY WATER

This one is for Jacob.

Corrupt

ADJECTIVE

Someone who is corrupt behaves in a way that is morally wrong, especially by doing dishonest or illegal things in return for money or power. — *Collins English Dictionary.*

"Power tends to corrupt and absolute power corrupts absolutely." — *Lord Acton*

"I think people are distrustful of politicians and are looking for someone who is telling the truth with no hidden agenda." — *Mohamed El Baradei*

PROLOGUE

ORANGE
NEW SOUTH WALES
2014

A sleek black Range Rover negotiated the white-gravel drive-way, its tires crunching as they passed over thousands of small, round pebbles. From within, looking out the heavily-tinted side window, was a well-dressed man with a clean-shaven square jaw. His dark hair and eyes gave the impression of a man in his thirties, but in fact, he was already into his forties.

Today would be the day, he thought. *Today I will set a new path and take care of a problem. Today.*

The man sighed. He despised killing, but in his business, it was a necessary evil.

Coming to a stop on an extensive roundabout, the vehicle parked in the shade of a large, double-story brick country man-sion with a wide balcony on the second floor. In the centre of the roundabout was a ring of small shrubs circling a fountain with a statue of a broad-winged angel in white marble, the angel's naked breast skewered by an arrow.

The man climbed out of the vehicle and stared at that arrow. *How ironic.*

Turning toward the house, he saw a tall man with a well-trimmed beard, who'd come out to greet him. Approaching the house, he met the man who'd started down the steps with his right hand outstretched; his jacket swinging open to reveal the Glock tucked in a shoulder holster. "Welcome home, sir."

The man nodded. "Thank you. Are they here?"

"Yes, sir."

"And all is prepared?"

"Yes, sir."

"Good. Let's do this, shall we?"

Double solid oak doors swung open and both men entered the large conference room, their strides purposeful. Before them, seated at a long rectangular table were three men. Like the two who'd just entered, they were similarly attired.

The room was well-lit by a combination of downlights and natural light pouring in through three large mullioned windows. Just outside the gleaming glazing was a hedge of LillyPillies, the tops of which were just visible. The floor was covered with a fine, soft and durable carpet made from one hundred percent Australian wool, while the walls boasted beautiful dark timber wainscoting.

The man smiled at those seated. "Welcome, gentlemen. I'm so glad you could come on such short notice."

"It didn't sound like we had much choice," grunted a thin-faced man in his early sixties.

"That's because you didn't. We must strike while the iron is hot or the opportunity to make millions will get away from us."

Now he had their attention.

"We already make millions," a second, more rotund man pointed out.

"We do. But this time we'll not need to import anything to do it. The substance we'll be using is right here in Australia. Let's call it a golden natural resource not made of gold."

"And that is?" asked the first man.

"Water."

The third man snorted derisively and shook his head, an action that didn't go unnoticed.

The man continued. "With the passing of the government's latest water bill through Parliament, it has opened the way for producers to buy and store all the water they need. They then have the option to sell it on at a healthy mark-up."

The second man was skeptical. "You're proposing that we buy and sell water?"

A smile lit their host's face. "No, gentlemen. My proposal is that we buy a cotton farm."

With the meeting now concluded, the three men began to file past their host. As the third man went to walk out, his path was blocked by the host's bodyguard who stood there shaking his head.

The third man gave him a look that radiated impatience and indignance and turned back to the host.

"What the hell is this?" he demanded.

"I wanted to have a chat with you without the others present."

"About what?"

"About the fact that you skimmed two million of the company's profits last year."

Alarm flared briefly in his eyes and then vanished. It was sufficient, however, to give him away. "I don't know what you're talking about."

It was a weak rebuttal and the host shook his head in disgust. "After all this time, Agostino, and this is how you treat our friendship."

Agostino stared at him in silence.

"Nothing to say? The director won't be happy."

Steel-hard eyes bored into Agostino along with an expression that seemed to last forever. A nervous tic developed at the corner of Agostino's left eye. Then it dropped to the corner of his mouth. He could withstand it no longer and shouted, "All right! I fucking did it. But it wasn't just me. OK? It wasn't just me."

A dull crump sounded in the distance and a glass of water on the polished tabletop vibrated.

The host nodded. "I know."

Agostino paled. "Oh God! Christ!"

"Time for you to go, Agostino."

Agostino's hands came up and clasped together in a pleading gesture. "No! No! Don't kill me."

He gave Agostino a wan smile. "I'm not going to kill you. But the next time I call you, you will answer. And you will do whatever I ask you to. Whatever I ask. If not, your wife, your daughter, even your sister, will all meet with unfortunate accidents."

The press was stopped at the gate. Vans with satellite dishes were parked haphazardly, taking up every square meter of space on the road shoulders. Television and newspaper reporters were crowded around like carrion eaters surrounding a piece of roadkill, fighting for any small morsel.

The coroner pushed the gurney containing the last of the two bodies into the back of his van and slammed the door. Moving to the driver's side door, he got in and drove down the drive, beeping his horn for the gate to be opened, allowing his exit from the crime scene.

Standing off to one side and deep in conversation were the fire chief and police chief superintendent from Orange. They separated and the fire chief returned to the charred wreck of the car, the police superintendent heading in the host's direction.

Stopping before him, the superintendent's face was etched with concern. He said, "The techs will go over what's left of the car and the surrounds with a fine-toothed comb, sir. I'm afraid we'll all be here for a few days yet until we're satisfied that we have collected every forensic trace."

"Take all the time you need."

The police officer stared towards the house, noticing a slim woman up on the balcony. Her long black hair was blowing in the breeze as she leaned against the rail, taking in the hive of activity. She wore tight-fitting jeans and a white singlet-top which hugged her large breasts.

"Your daughter?" the superintendent asked.

The man turned to look. "My wife."

More than a little red-faced, the police officer turned back to face the wreck. "You don't get out here much, do you?"

"Only when I want to get away from it all."

"We're pretty sure it was some type of bomb. You wouldn't have any idea who'd want to do something like this, would you?"

The man turned and stared hard into the superintendent's eyes. "As a matter of fact, I would."

Ten minutes later, the superintendent finished writing in his notebook, thanked the host and walked back across to the fire chief who was standing beside and staring at the wreckage. He looked at the police officer and asked, "How did you go?"

"He gave us a lead."

"Oh?"

"Yeah, we'll just have to see if it pans out."

The superintendent turned his head to look back at the

host who was talking on a phone. Then he shifted his gaze up to the balcony. The woman was gone.

CHAPTER ONE

If Ray Petersen failed to make the river, he'd die. It was that simple, and the knowledge spurred him on. He'd seen something he wasn't meant to and gone to investigate further, realizing now that it was a stupid idea and he should have just reported it instead.

His legs felt like lead as they pumped up and down like pistons in a motor. Every breath he drew was harder than the last, and his heart felt like it was going to explode and create a great hole in his chest. Oh man, he wanted to lay down. Christ, how he wanted to lay down.

A low branch from a young Rivergum whipped across his face, opening a shallow gash in his sweat-stained cheek. The instant burn of salt-laden fluid biting raw flesh made him wince, but he had no time to wipe it away.

His feet pawed the air as the ground dropped away from beneath him, and he fell forward into a shallow gully. Ray crashed hard into the bottom of the dry creek bed, and his face hit, his mouth filling with red dirt. Crying out in despair, he dragged himself to his feet once more.

With grim determination, he clawed his way up the opposite bank and continued to make his stumbling way further through the scrub. The red dirt clung to his lower legs, blending with the sweat and blood that ran from multiple cuts and abrasions.

Behind him, he could hear voices, much louder this time. His pursuers were closing in, which meant that his death was imminent if he didn't reach his boat. He stopped and looked at the sky. The fiery orange orb was slightly higher than the western horizon. If he could just avoid them until it was dark, then he could get to his boat.

Ray's head twisted right and left, his desperation peaking. He needed to find somewhere to hide.

"There he is!"

The excited shout reached his ears and Ray turned and looked through the trees and saw a man with a rifle up to his shoulder. The weapon fired and the bullet made a distinctive crack as it passed close to his head.

Ducking instinctively, Ray turned to run and got hooked up on a branch. It ripped his dirty, sweat-stained blue shirt and scored his skin. He ground his teeth together against the sharp pain and kept going.

Another shot. This one cut through a small branch to his

right which fell to the ground. Ray jumped to the left and stumbled, gathered himself, then ran on.

Just ahead, a line of great Rivergums loomed, indicating that he'd made the river. Relief. It was enough to release a last surge of adrenaline to get him across the line. Now, if he could just get into the boat, he could get the hell out of there and report it to the police.

"For fuck's sake, shoot the prick!" a voice hollered. "Don't let him get away."

Two shots this time. One flew harmlessly wide while the second ripped through the fabric, gouged out flesh, then drove deep into the trunk of a huge Rivergum.

Ray cried out and lost his footing. He fell forward into empty space before finally crashing to earth halfway down the steep riverbank. Rolling in a tangle of arms and legs, hitting every part of his body as he went, he came to an abrupt stop at the water's edge. Groaning, Ray went to sit up and felt his ribs give.

"Christ Jesus," he moaned.

Trying again, desperate to keep moving, more pain ripped through his left side. He ground his teeth together and managed to get unsteadily to his feet. The boat was only a couple of meters to his left. Ray grasped the rope he'd attached to a fallen branch and pulled it free. Lurching towards the boat, he fell over the side as he tried to get in. The vessel rocked violently and pushed away from the bank.

Ray hissed as his busted ribs contacted with the tinnie's aluminum seat. For a moment he thought he was going to blackout as his vision blurred and objects swam before his eyes. Taking a deep breath, he gathered himself and moved to the back of the boat where the motor was. Fiddling with it briefly, he pulled the starter.

"Fuck!" he screeched in pain as bone grated on bone. Again, his vision blurred. The outboard had refused to fire so he had to do it again.

Ray set his jaw firm and raised his arm to wipe the sweat from his brow with the back of his hand. Tugging the starter again, he bit back another profanity at the pain it had caused but was relieved when the motor kicked to life with a puff of blue smoke. He grasped the throttle and gave it a savage twist. As the propeller bit into the murky brown water of the Barwon River, Ray turned the boat's nose to point upriver towards the small town of Collari.

The bow on the tinnie came up and the roar of the engine crescendoed to a peak before it had gone fifty meters.

Fighting back tears of relief and pain, Ray made a silent promise to his wife that he'd resign his damned job when he got back.

Behind him, on top of the riverbank above the Barwon, four men with rifles watched the tinnie disappear around a bend further up. Their leader reached behind his back and retrieved a satellite phone. Punching in some numbers, he put it to his ear.

"Yeah. It's me. We've got a problem."

COLLARI
7.12 PM

It was after dark when Ray bashed on the door of the Collari Police Station. The light was on so he knew that someone had to be about. He hammered his fist on the door again and it shuddered with each blow.

His whole body ached, his ribs hurt like a bitch and he was covered in scratches and dried blood. Not to mention the wound where he'd been shot.

Pounding on the door again, he kept up a continuous beat until it swung open, and he was faced with an angry middle-aged man sporting a mustache and a uniform.

"Where's the damned fire?" he growled. Then he saw the condition Ray was in. "Shit, what happened to you?"

Ray pushed past him and said, "They tried to kill me."

"What?" the police sergeant said and swung the door shut. "Who tried to kill you?"

Ray winced and found a chair to sit on. He gasped as his ribs grated once more, and said, "Out at Dawn Station. I was checking the water meters on the pumps."

The sergeant raised his eyebrows. "You're an inspector?"

Ray nodded. "Ray Petersen. Listen, I need a doctor. I've got busted ribs and the bastards shot me."

"They shot you?"

He showed the officer the wound.

"OK."

The sergeant retrieved a phone from his pocket and

speed dialed a number. He waited for a few heartbeats before somebody answered and he said, "Yeah, this is Sergeant Chris Royall. I've got a bloke here at the station who's pretty banged up. Needs some attention."

He waited again and then, "See you soon."

Hanging up, he said, "He'll be here soon."

Ray nodded. "Are you on your own?"

"Yes. My constable is out on patrol. Won't be back for a couple of hours."

Ray looked around the waiting area. His gaze stopped at the corkboard with several faded posters of wanted felons on it. He was sure he recognized one of them. Malcolm Naden. But he'd been caught some time back. Obviously, it had been overlooked. The counter was set back against a wall and unlike some of those he'd seen, was missing the Perspex that dropped down from the ceiling.

"Did you hear me, Ray?"

He looked back at Royall. "Huh?"

"What were you doing?"

"It was the last one I had to do. I stopped to check the pumps and water meter attached to them. The pumps were working but the meter had been disconnected. Those things pump billions of liters of water and the lion's share goes to Dawn Station. But what I saw—"

He paused as pain washed over him, then continued, "I saw that their water storages were all full. So, the question is, where does the water that they are pumping, go?"

"I guess they sell it on down the river to other stations," the police officer suggested.

Ray thought for a moment. "The bastards can make more money that way. Especially if they hang on to it until the next drought sets in. They would make hundreds of millions. But it doesn't tell me where they store it all."

There was a knock at the door to the station.

Royall said, "That'll be the doctor."

CHAPTER TWO

ONE WEEK LATER
SYDNEY MIRROR, TUESDAY

Canberra: *Reports yesterday from an inside source have indicated that independent Senator Colin Worth is to put forth a motion this week for limits to what water landowners can store on their properties in Northern New South Wales and in Western Queensland.*

This comes about after an in-depth report on the ABC's Four Corners show several months ago which exposed some of the owners of the mega-stations who are flouting the laws laid out by the water commission.

The Mirror is still waiting for the Water Minister to comment.

CANBERRA
9.45 AM

Detective Sergeant Gloria Browning of the Australian Federal Police threw the newspaper onto the top of her cluttered
desktop and let out a long breath. The report in the paper was
sure to shake a few trees and rattle a few cages. Especially in
Canberra.

There was a knock on her office door and a detective senior
constable wearing a dark suit entered the room. He glanced
around at the mess and smiled, "You know, you might clean
up every now and then."

"Shut up and tell me what you want, Leroy," Gloria
snapped.

"You read the paper?"

"Yep."

"What do you think?"

"I think it'll get somebody's attention."

Dark-haired Leroy Mertens sat down in a battered chair on
the other side of her desk. "Do you think it will be enough to
get an operation green-light?"

Gloria paused. She and her team had been trying for the
past two months to get an operation allowed to investigate
what was happening with the water commission. Ever since
the Four Corners' report. What the report hadn't aired on
television was the fact that there was corruption in the government somewhere, but no one knew where. Hence the need
for the op. They required wiretaps and an undercover for

work out west.

Having done some groundwork already, she'd spoken to several people within the Murray Darling Basin Authority, who checked the pumps and meters that the properties used. Some of the reports disturbed her. Inspectors were being intimidated, one had been assaulted, and others had received death threats. And nothing was being done about it.

She shrugged. "Who knows."

The phone on her desk rang. Somewhere beneath the mountain of paperwork. Leaning forward, she shuffled some of the mess around to find it, with papers and folders falling to the floor. "Fuck it."

Leroy grimaced. "Paperwork isn't your strong suit is it, boss?"

"I wish I'd never taken this damn job."

Finally, she found the phone and lifted the receiver. "Browning."

Listening intently to the person on the other end, she said very little in return until the end of the brief conversation. "All right, Hugh, I'll give someone at New South Wales Police a call."

Gloria hung up. Reaching up to the back of her head, she undid the bun in her hair, letting her blonde locks, all wavy from being tied up since wet, fall past her shoulders so that it framed her fine-featured face. Leroy stared at her and couldn't help but think how hot his boss really was.

"Shit, shit, shit!" Gloria growled and banged her palm on the messy desktop.

"What is it?" Leroy asked.

"One of the water commission inspectors has disappeared."

Leroy leaned forward in the chair. "When?"

"A week ago."

"Shit."

"Exactly."

CHAPTER THREE

Senator Colin Worth finished the last of his lukewarm coffee and pulled a face at the bitter taste of it. He crossed to the kitchen sink in the small unit he used while in Canberra for sitting days and rinsed the cup out. Once it was reasonably clean, he placed it upside down in the dish rack and went back to the paperwork he had spread out across the table.

His briefcase open, he began to place the files in it, straightening some of the wayward sheets as he went. He looked up when Romana appeared in the doorway. Her hair was disheveled and all she had on was one of his business shirts. The forty-year-old parliamentarian turned to face her. Staring at her long, tanned legs, he loved the graceful way they moved when she walked, and he felt a stirring inside.

She stopped in front of him and pressed her body against his. Running a long-fingered hand through his dark hair to the back of his head, she pulled it forward until their lips met.

When they broke apart, she smiled and said, "Good morning."

Worth smiled. "Yes, indeed."

"Are you ready for today?"

"Yes. I have everything I need."

"You'll get my vote, Senator," she said seductively.

"Why, thank you, Senator."

Pressing herself against him once more, she whispered, "What would they say if word got out that you were screwing the leader of the Greens?"

Worth chuckled, "They would say, what a lucky lady you are, Senator Romana Fielding."

She punched him playfully on the shoulder. He, in turn, reached around and pinched her right buttock cheek. "Get in the shower. I'll wait for you."

"Don't bother. I have a few calls to make. I'll see you there. Besides, what would the rumor mill say?"

"You do realize that there are reporters outside already? They've been there since six."

"All the more reason for you to get out of here," Romana told him.

Worth nodded. "Fair enough."

She disappeared into the bathroom and Worth finished packing his briefcase. Before leaving, he poked his head into the bathroom. The room was full of steam and the mirror had fogged up, so he couldn't use its reflective surface to catch one final glimpse of Romana's naked form as she washed it.

He called out, "I'm off now."

Putting her head around the corner, her wet hair hung straggly across her exposed shoulder, and she blew him a kiss. "Bye."

Worth closed the door and picked up his briefcase from the table. Exiting the unit, he walked down an internal staircase and into the parking garage where his driver awaited him.

"Morning, Len. How's the wife doing?"

The bearded chauffer smiled as he opened the rear door on the passenger side. "She's feeling a lot better today, Mr. Worth."

"Great to hear."

Len closed the door behind him and walked around the front of the white Holden Commodore and climbed into the driver's seat. Putting the key into the ignition, he looked at his boss in the rear-view mirror. "Are we stopping anywhere before work today, sir?"

"Not this morning, Len."

He turned the key and the engine came to life. While the motor idled, Len put his seatbelt on and then selected drive.

The car went up the ramp and out through a secure gate. It was immediately mobbed by the waiting press trying to get pictures, or hoping the car would stop and the senator would field some questions. But it didn't and the car turned right, heading towards the center of the capital.

It had traveled no further than a hundred meters when it

happened. In a bright flash of orange and with a resounding crump, the car blew up, the concussive blast smashing windows in the area as well as setting off car alarms. A black pall of smoke billowed into the air as debris rained down.

Back in the unit, Romana Fielding rushed naked and wet to the window that overlooked the street. When she realized what had happened, she placed a trembling hand to her open mouth to stifle the heart-wrenching screams that were forthcoming at the sight of her lover's burning car.

CHAPTER FOUR

CANBERRA
A SHORT TIME LATER

The door to Gloria's office burst open, startling her. She gathered herself and stared at the form of Leroy filling the void. "Christ, Leroy. Have you ever heard about knocking?"

"Someone just killed Senator Colin Worth," he blurted out, the excitement evident in his eyes.

"What?"

"Whoever it was, they blew up his car. Killed him and his driver."

"Bloody hell."

"Exactly."

She thought for a moment and rose to her feet. "Come with me."

They left her office and walked along a short hallway to her commanding officer's office. Knocking once, she swung the door open.

Commander Pete Hoyland sat watching the flat-screen television on his wall while talking to someone on the phone.

Hoyland was in his fifties with grey hair and a round face; too much desk work, he complained.

Once he was finished, Hoyland said, "I see you've heard."

"Yes, sir."

"And I suppose you're here to tell me that it has something to do with his proposed water bill?"

"Seems to be mighty coincidental, sir."

"I agree. So do the higher-ups."

"Now will you green-light the op, sir?"

"I still need to talk to a few people about it, but I should be able to convince them to let you run it."

"Good."

"Do you still have that crazy idea about your undercover?"

Gloria nodded.

"Do you think he'll go for it?"

"You get the op cleared, sir, and I'll get the undercover."

"Give me until the end of the day."

"Yes, sir."

They left Hoyland's office, and once they were out in the hallway, Leroy asked, "What do you mean you'll get the undercover? I thought I would do this."

Gloria shook her head. "Not this one, Leroy. I want a man with special skills on this."

"And I haven't," he asked, offended.

"Yes, you do. But you're not the person I want. It's nothing personal."

"Then who have you got in mind?"

"Dave Nash."

Surprise registered on Leroy's face. "The undercover who cracked up and took down the hierarchy of the Outback Animals?"

They reached Gloria's office and she closed the door behind them. Her stare fixed on Leroy and she said, "He didn't crack up."

"Not what I heard."

"They were going to kill him and he managed to take a gun off one of them. He put out the lights of a few before he was safe. His backup was late, and one of them actually worked for the bikers and tried to kill their boss outside the clubhouse in a van. After that, he quit."

Leroy gave her a questioning look. "How do you know so much?"

"Because I was there."

"No shit?"

"Yeah. Now that's out of the way, I want you to get on top of this bombing thing, just in case we get the go-ahead."

"Right on it."

At three o'clock that afternoon, the door to Gloria's office opened and Hoyland's head appeared in the opening. She was in the middle of trying to limit the disarray of her desktop. He said, "You're good to go, Gloria. They ticked it off."

Gloria couldn't help but show her excitement. "Yes."

Hoyland stepped into the room. His face was set with a hard expression. "It took some convincing for them to accept using an outsider as an undercover. Especially one with his reputation and history. Don't let him fuck it up."

"He'll be fine, sir. He's damned good."

"He's also been out of the game for the past few years," Hoyland pointed out.

Gloria remained silent.

"Also, the higher-ups want to be kept constantly in the loop. You'll need to catch up on the investigation so far from Morris' team. I want reports from you every day. I take it that you'll head up the investigative team this end, and have some-one out there as back up for your boy?"

"No. I mean yes."

"Which is it, no or yes?"

"I'll head up the team this end, but there will be no second person with Nash. That's why I want him. He operates better autonomously."

"That's a damn fine way to get him killed."

"Trust me, sir. If he needs help, he'll ask for it. Besides, we can have a team on the ground out there in a few hours. Too many new faces in a small town will draw too much attention."

Hoyland sighed. "I sure hope you know what you're doing."

Gloria picked up a piece of paper from her desk. "I have a list of requests here, sir, if you would like to take a look at it?"

Hoyland took the list and ran a critical eye over it. He looked at Gloria and said, "I think I can manage this. Most of it, anyway."

"Thank you, sir."

"However, signed blank warrants might be a stretch."

"They would be handy, sir. Especially if we have to act on something fast. Sometimes waiting around for a judge just seems to fuck everything up."

He gave her a wry smile. "Just make sure *you* don't fuck everything up."

"Yes, sir."

Hoyland disappeared out the door and Gloria played paper shuffle until she found her phone. Picking up the handset, she pushed a button. Leroy answered on the other end. "Get your arse in here."

Within a minute, Leroy was there.

"What's up?"

"We've been given the green-light. You need to inform the rest of the team and get up to speed with Morris' team. By the time I get back, I want to know everything you do. From what explosives were used, to what the senator had for breakfast. Understood?"

"Roger."

"I'll be back by tomorrow night at the latest."

"Where are you going?"

"Sydney, to get Nash."

"Mighty inconvenient isn't it? We're just taking off and you're flying the coop."

"That's why I'm leaving it in your capable hands. And put a bomb under the tech guys."

Leroy winced.

"Too soon?"

"Yeah."

CHAPTER FIVE

... and police still have no leads as to those responsible for the death of Senator Colin Worth who was killed this morning when his car blew up. All that is known is that an explosive device was used ...

"Yeah, yeah, whatever," Nash grumbled, stabbing a finger at the button to turn the car radio off.

Raising his binoculars to his eyes, he focussed on the house across the road. The front curtains were open, and he could see the couple sitting at the dining room table, sipping wine and making goo-goo eyes at each other.

The man reached out his hand and the woman did the same. They met halfway and clasped them together.

"Christ," Nash groaned. How many more hours would he have to do this shit? The wife already knew the bastard was having an affair with his secretary. It was always the secretary. Yet she wanted more. What more could he give her?

The man's name was Lyle Henderson. He was a lawyer in a big firm based in the inner-city. The woman was his junior secretary, junior to him by twenty years. Her name was Mary Smith.

Nash had been watching them for the past month. Charging a flat rate of five hundred dollars per day, he'd already made a tidy sum off it. And all he had to do was watch them eat, drink, and fuck. And did they give rabbits a run for their money?

For the last two years, this was pretty much his life as a private investigator, and he'd had enough. The interesting cases were few and far between. In fact, they were bloody non-existent.

Lowering the binoculars, he reached for the thermos on the passenger seat and poured himself another cup of coffee and placed the flask next to the Canon camera with its 70-200mm zoom lens.

Taking a sip from the cup, he picked the binoculars back up to look. He cursed, "Frigging hell, not again."

In the time it had taken for him to pour the coffee, the couple had discarded most of their clothing and were now at it on the dining room table. The secretary was perched on the edge with her legs wrapped around the waist of her lawyer Casanova, whose pants were down around his ankles and his shirt discarded. His face was buried between her ample breasts.

Mary's fingers dug into his shoulders and her head was tossed back in her throes of pleasure, her long dark hair touching the table behind her.

Suddenly, Nash was aware of the door beside him being wrenched opened and the influx of cool air from outside. A voice snarled, "Got you, arsehole!" and before he knew it, Nash was being dragged from the car.

Spilling his coffee on his jeans, he swore as he tried to break free of his attacker. "What the fuck are you doing, buddy? Piss off!"

"I'll give you piss off, Nash, and I'm not your buddy!" the man spat and swung a hard right at the PI before he could straighten up his six-one frame.

The blow hit Nash just above his left ear and lights flashed in front of his eyes. Staggering, he caught himself on the side of his battered BA Falcon before he went down. Another blow mashed his lips and blood flooded his mouth.

"How'd you like that, you son of a bitch?" his attacker bellowed.

Nash straightened up and shook his head. He looked through the fog in his eyes and saw a large man standing before him. At least he understood why those first blows hurt.

"Are you ready for some more?"

Nash blinked the face into focus. "Harry Bowers?"

"One and the same, arsehole. You ruined my life. Now I'm going to do the same to you."

Harry Bowers was one of Nash's early cases. Another one where the husband was screwing the secretary. Except with this one, the wife held all the cards, and when she left, she cleaned him out to the tune of twenty million.

"Not my fault you couldn't keep your dick in your pants," Nash said.

"Yeah, well I'm going to cut yours off," Bowers snarled.

Until then, Nash hadn't noticed the large knife in the man's right hand. "You don't want to do that, Harry."

"Why not? I've got nothing to lose."

Not really wanting to take his eyes from the maniac in front of him, the PI risked a glance across the road and in through the window. Mary and Lyle were still at it, totally oblivious of what was happening out on the street.

Fat lot of good you are.

Harry closed in and swung the knife back and forth. Nash jumped back out of reach.

"Stop this shit, Harry. Before someone gets hurt."

"You're the only prick around here that'll get hurt," he snapped. "I'm going to cut you so bad your guts will spill."

"Couldn't you just shoot me? I hate knives."

Harry closed the distance between them and slashed back and forth like he was wielding a machete. Nash was able to avoid the strokes with ease but if it kept up, there was a chance the crazed bastard would get lucky.

Harry drew back again and snarled, "Keep fucking still so I can kill you already."

"Last chance, Harry. Stop this shit or I'm going to hurt you."

"Fuck you."

He came in hard, knife low as he tried to gut Nash where he stood. But the PI was ready for him and moved to the left and then drove his right fist into Harry's rage-etched face.

The blow rocked the big man to his core. While he was stunned, Nash chopped down on his wrist. The hand went numb, releasing the knife. It fell to the road with a clatter.

Next Nash hit him again. A blow which broke Harry's nose, causing blood to spurt all over the man's shirt. Grasping at the ruined appendage, he staggered back.

The PI moved in close and kicked the bigger man in the nuts. With a high-pitched squeak, Harry dropped to his knees, clutching at his crotch.

Nash stood in front of him and stared down at the pale but bloody face. "I warned you, Harry. I told you what would happen."

"Fuck … you," he squeaked.

Nash hit him again and Harry Bowers fell onto his side and didn't move.

Blowing hard, he stared back at the window across the street and cursed. They were gone.

Nash heard footsteps behind him, and a voice said, "My, how the mighty have fallen. There was a time you would have shot him."

He turned and stared at the speaker. "Cops like you won't let me have a gun. They think I'm too unstable."

Gloria stepped from the shadows and into the dim illumination thrown by the street light. Nash drew a sharp breath. She wore her hair long, and her blue jeans tight. On top was an unzipped brown coat, revealing a white blouse beneath.

"Happens like that sometimes," she admitted.

"Seems to me that whenever someone is trying to kill me,

you happen to be standing there watching."

"You looked like you had it under control."

Nash wiped the blood from his mouth and spit on the road. "Cut the shit, Gloria. I haven't seen you for two years. What do you want?"

Gloria studied him in the dim light, not that she had to because she could see that he hadn't changed. Not since the time they had spent together. Six-two, solid, brown eyes, unshaven jawline, wavy brown hair. "Got a job for you."

He turned away. "Piss off."

"You're not going to listen to what I have to say, Dave?"

"No."

"I need a good undercover, Dave."

"You've got your own team. Use one of them."

Gloria hesitated. "How do you...?"

"It doesn't matter. I quit, remember? The police force isn't going to have me back."

"I've already had it cleared, Dave. If you want, you're in."

Nash opened the door of his car and looked back at her. "Have you got wheels?"

"Yes."

"I assume that since you found me here, you know where I live?"

"Uh-huh."

"See you there," he said and climbed inside the Falcon.

CHAPTER SIX

CANBERRA
10:31 PM

Leroy Mertens sat at his desk, watching the grainy security vision provided by the house across the road from Worth's unit. It wasn't much but it was all they had. He and others in Gloria's team had questioned witnesses, canvassed the houses along the street and no one had seen anything. Even the security cameras in the unit block where Worth had lived didn't work.

It was by chance they'd stumbled across what they had. The system in question had an automatic overwrite on a one-week cycle. As luck would have it, they had the previous five days.

So far, he'd gone through three of those five but found nothing.

"Have you found anything, yet?"

Leroy looked up and saw Constable Annie Long standing in the doorway of his office. She was in her mid-twenties with red hair and freckles. She also had the most mesmerizing green eyes Leroy had ever seen.

"Not so far," he said.

"Want some company?"

He gave her a tired smile. "Sure, why not?"

She pulled a chair over and sat beside him so she could see the monitor, and grimaced. "That sure is a shit picture."

"Not wrong," Leroy agreed. "What did you find out on the hill?"

She snorted. "I found out that those pricks up there can spin shit so thick that by the time they're finished, they even believe what comes out."

Leroy smiled. "Nothing, I take it then."

"All they're concerned about are opinion polls. Sure, they're shocked that it was one of their own, but at the moment they're concentrating on the rumors that there could be a spill motion for the leadership of the Labour Party and the Prime Minister could be ousted and replaced by the end of next week."

Leroy looked at her. "Really? What tosser are they going to get to replace him?"

"The Water Minister."

"This is the last thing he'd want on his doorstep."

"I'd say."

"Did someone question Romana Fielding?"

"I did. Can't believe that those two were doing horizontal calisthenics for the past twelve months and no one knew."

"Could she enlighten you any?"

"Nope. She was in the shower when the car blew. Same

with the driver's wife. She couldn't help us any either. He'd worked for Worth since 2012. By all reports, they got on well. When will the bomb tech's report be in?"

Leroy sighed. "Preliminary one should be tomorrow. At least it'll give us somewhere to start."

Silence descended over the pair for a few minutes as they watched the grainy images before them.

Annie asked, "When is the boss back?"

"She said tomorrow."

"Is it true?"

"What?"

"She's bringing in Dave Nash to go undercover."

"Yes."

"Shit. That guy is a legend."

"He's a loose cannon."

"What he did to those bikies is talked about everywhere in the halls of law enforcement."

Leroy slumped back in his seat. "This is a waste of fucking time."

Annie asked, "Where are you up to?"

"The night before last."

"You're almost done then."

"I still have last night's vision to go through," Leroy pointed out.

Annie shook her head. "Nope. That *would* be a waste of time. The car wasn't there last night. The driver had it at his place. He takes it home once a week to give it a good detail."

Leroy almost exploded out of his chair. "What? Why

wasn't I told?"

"I thought you knew. He takes it home once a week on the same night. Regular as clockwork."

"Christ! Get people out there tomorrow and canvass the whole street. Find out if anybody saw anything or has CCTV footage we can use. Whoever did this didn't do it at the unit. They did it at the driver's home. Get some crime-scene guys over there as well. I can't believe I wasn't fucking told. Gloria will hit the roof."

CHAPTER SEVEN

Nash flicked the light switch on as he walked through the front door to his unit and said, "You'll have to excuse the mess, sorry. The cleaner has the week off."

Gloria smiled as she closed the door. There was shit everywhere and she gave her nose a slight wrinkle. "Don't be. It reminds me of my office."

He tossed his keys onto the table. They skidded across the only bare patch and onto the floor. "You want a beer?"

"Sure. Why not?"

Nash opened the fridge and Gloria caught a glimpse of the interior. Two six-packs of VB and a pizza box. She winced.

He grabbed two beers and closed the door, then walked across the cluttered room and handed her the beer. "Take a seat."

Gloria looked around the room for one. The lounge was covered in papers and the one and only chair looked as though it had a load of dirty washing on it.

Nash saw the expression on her face and said, "Sorry." Then he walked to the lounge and scooped everything onto the floor. "There, all good."

Gloria removed her coat, then sat down and twisted the top off her beer while Nash pushed the clothes off the chair. "Must wash them one of these days."

Not one to hold her tongue at times, Gloria took a pull on the beer and then let out what was going through her mind. "What the fuck are you doing, Dave? This isn't you. What happened to that switched-on guy I knew? You're a fucking slob."

Nash's eyes flared. "I'm not him anymore, Gloria."

"Well obviously," she indicated with her hand. "But you could be. Come work for me and get out of this shithole."

"I already told you, I don't do that work anymore."

"Yes, you did. And I cry bullshit, Dave."

"You could cry rivers of blood for all I care, Gloria, and the answer would still be the same."

"You're a stubborn arsehole, Dave Nash. Tell me something. How's business? Do you get the same buzz looking through windows and watching people fuck? Is it like the one you got when you were undercover, knowing that one slip could be your last?"

Nash's voice was laced with sarcasm. "Says she who's riding a desk."

Gloria came to her feet. "I had no fucking choice! It's safer for my daughter that way."

The PI wasn't about to stop. "Oh yes. Your daughter Rachel. How old is she? Two? I have been meaning to ask you about her."

Her voice took on a caustic edge. "Don't you dare, Dave Nash."

Immediately he knew he'd gone too far and tried to repair the damage. "I'm sorry, Gloria. I shouldn't have said anything like that."

"No, you shouldn't have," she snapped. "I have to go. This was a mistake."

He could see the hurt in her eyes as she stood up.

"Wait, Gloria."

She placed the beer bottle on the cluttered bench-top and moved towards her coat. Nash came to his feet and cut her off. "Wait."

Her eyes glistened. "Get out of my way."

She went to step around him and he blocked her path again. He said, "No."

She slapped him hard.

Grabbing her arms, he pulled her close, crushing her lips with his. Gloria fought it for all of two heartbeats before succumbing to the situation and responded, returning the kiss.

They broke apart and she slapped him again.

Surprised, Nash asked, "What was that for."

"*That* was for being an arsehole."

He stared into Gloria's blue eyes and couldn't help but be

mesmerized by them.

"What?" she asked.

He let her go and stepped back. "Nothing. Just remember-ing."

Gloria reached down and grabbed her coat. She put it on and walked towards the door without looking back. A million thoughts ran through Nash's head and he opened his mouth to speak. "Molly."

Gloria stopped and stiffened. She hesitated before turning to face him. "What did you call me?"

"Gloria, stay."

Her shoulders slumped. "I can't."

"Well, then tell me one thing before you go. Please?"

She stared at him but remained silent.

"Is she mine? Is Rachel mine?"

"You know where to find me."

And Gloria was gone.

CHAPTER EIGHT

KATANKA
OUTBACK NEW SOUTH WALES
2016

Nash was fucked. Meat was bashing the shit out of him and there was no backup to be seen. Once they'd found the wire he was wearing he knew he was screwed. Now he was surrounded by the entire Outback Animals outlaw motorcycle gang in their clubhouse. A bad bunch of killers involved in organized crime, who did everything from drugs, human trafficking, prostitution, and racketeering.

"I heard you were a fucking cop, Nash," Meat snarled into his face. "I guess it pays to have someone on the inside. Your friend has been very reliable."

"Which one?"

Meat just smiled.

He'd told his bosses it was a fucking bad idea. But that stuck-

up arsehole Warren wouldn't listen. It was probably him.

"The police minister wants this wrapped up," the bald little fuck had said. "He says it's been going on too long. Costing too much money. So, get these bastards on tape, and do it yesterday."

Dave Nash was an undercover detective who worked under the Taskforce Hammerhead banner. The brief of the team was to take down organized crime wherever they found it. This time it happened to be the Outback Animals Motorcycle Club.

He'd been undercover for the best part of twelve months, putting his life on the line for the task force, and now when he needed them, where the fuck were they?

Nash had stared at the crowd through the red haze and seen Gloria. Only she wasn't Gloria then. The Animals called her Molly. Nothing else, just Molly.

Now it was all coming apart. Meat sneered at him as he took out his Glock 19 which was stuffed in his belt. He raised it and placed it against Nash's forehead and hissed, "Goodnight, motherfucker."

"The wire's been dead for five minutes. We need to get in there."

"Just wait," Joe Warren said in a calm voice. "Nash knows what he's doing."

"Damn it, Joe, we're all he's got since the arseholes higher up pulled the money and manpower off this thing."

"I said wait, Red."

Red Kelly wasn't happy. He'd wanted to go as soon as the

wire went dead, but Warren had ordered him to stay put and not blow Nash's cover. He needed to get in there.

"Fuck it! I'm going. I'm not spending one more minute in this sweatbox," he snarled and tossed the headphones aside.

"Sit down!" Warren roared.

With swift movements, Red pulled his personal weapon and brought it into line with his boss.

"What the hell—"

Warren reacted with a swiftness that belied his forty-seven years. His left hand came up and knocked the hand with the gun in it towards the roof of the van. It discharged immediately and blew a hole through the lining and out into the daylight. The sound was deafening in the confined space, making their ears ring.

Warren chopped his right hand across Red's throat, stunning him. Then he drove his hand beneath his coat and brought out his own police-issue weapon.

"You didn't just do that, you fuck!" BLAM. "Fuck you!" BLAM, BLAM.

Red jerked under every impact as the three rounds slammed into him. His eyes sprang wide and his jaw dropped. Then the light in his eyes started to fade as death claimed him.

When he started to slump, Warren pushed the body away.

Then realisation hit Warren like a bolt of lightning. "Shit! Nash."

He thrust open the door of the van and bright sunlight assailed his eyes. He blinked twice and leaped out, the heat of the day slapping him in the face.

That's when the gunfire erupted from inside the clubhouse. "Christ!" Warren cursed and started to run.

It was the muffled reports that saved Nash's life. It gave him the distraction he needed.

Meat's head swiveled, and in that instant, Nash brought up his hands so fast they were a blur.

He wrapped them around the Glock and twisted savagely. The wrist broke and the fingers on the biker's right hand released the weapon. Nash reversed it and shot Meat in the head.

The head snapped back and the gang leader fell like a tree.

Without waiting to see the final result, he pivoted and dropped the Glock's foresight on the closest barrel-chested gorilla covered in tattoos who was bringing up a handgun in a meaty fist when the Glock spat lead at him. Nash fired twice and both rounds burned into the man's chest.

The giant staggered, lurching forward, so the undercover detective shot him again.

Nash, once more bloody and bruised, moved, no, lurched to his left and shot another biker. This one screamed out in pain and collapsed in an untidy heap.

Suddenly he felt arms wrap around him, his own pinned at his sides. Struggling to break free, he found he couldn't. Hot, fetid breath assaulted his left ear, and Nash moved his head forward and then back with one swift motion.

Stars flashed before his eyes as his head connected with that of the biker. He felt the grip loosen and he twisted, bringing up the Glock and burying it deep in the flesh under the biker's chin.

Nash fired twice and both slugs punched out of the top of the man's skull. Dropping at the undercover's feet, the body lay still, blood pooling from the ghastly wound.

Nash turned in a circle, the gun moving with him. His bloody lips twisted in a snarl and he almost roared, "Who's fucking next?"

Then his gaze settled on Molly.

"All right, arseholes! Nobody fucking move!"

Nash shook his head. Fucking Warren.

"Gloria Browning, Australian Federal Police, People Smuggling Taskforce."

Nash stared up at her from where he sat on the rear tailgate of the ambulance while the grey-haired paramedic dabbed at one of his many cuts. The undercover shook his head. "Shit, this day just keeps getting better."

The woman he knew as Molly, nodded. "You handled yourself well in there."

A wave of anger washed over Nash as he stared into her eyes and remembered the nights they had screwed each other senseless. All an act. From both of them. They'd played each other.

"It was nice of you to help me in there," his voice dripped with sarcasm.

She shrugged. "No sense in both of our covers being blown."

"Did you know?"

"That you were a cop?"

"Yeah."

She shook her head. "Did you?"

"No."

"Someone is going to be pissed."

Gloria nodded. "Two years of work gone, just like that."

"Here comes trouble," Nash said.

Gloria turned and saw Warren. The man's head seemed to be shrouded in a grey cloud from the shit storm that was brewing inside him. He stopped in front of them both but his anger was directed at the Federal officer.

"What the fuck are you lot doing here without so much as a fucking courtesy call? Talk about great communication between agencies."

"We didn't know you had an agent on the inside."

"That's what a damned phone is for. Ever tried to use one?"

"Easy, Warren. It isn't her fault."

Warren's eyes flared. "You would say that. You were screwing her."

Nash came to his feet. A spark ignited inside. "Fuck you, Warren. Take your shit somewhere else. I've had about all I'm going to take from you. Back away before I do something you'll regret."

"Are you threatening me, you son of a bitch? A superior officer?"

"Damned straight."

All around them people had stopped to stare. Police, ambos,

crime scene techs. Gloria glanced about and then said, "Easy, boys. People are watching your little display."

Warren's head snapped around. "I don't give two shits who sees. So, shut your damned hole. This doesn't concern you. I'm still his damned boss."

Gloria held up her hands and backed away.

"Not anymore you aren't," Nash snapped.

"What?"

"I quit. Stick your job up your arse."

"You can't do that," Warren shot back.

"I just did," Nash snarled and stormed off.

"This isn't finished, Nash!" Warren shouted after him.

Nash replied in the only way left to him. He flipped him the finger.

"Oh, Christ!" Gloria exclaimed and threw her head back as another orgasm washed over her. The head of the motel bed bashed on the wall behind it from Nash's powerful thrusts. Sweat dripped from his brow onto her large, rose-tipped breasts.

The undercover built towards his own climax and grunted with an animalistic ferocity. Then, he too threw his own head back and cried out as he released his pent-up frustration inside her.

He rolled off Gloria and lay there. Staring up at the ceiling fan that made lazy circles above them, he could see a thick layer of dust on every blade.

Gloria moved beside him and rolled to her left to get her cigarettes. Unconcerned about the no-smoking sticker on the wall, she lit one and took a deep pull from it. The smoke flowed deep into her lungs, and as she exhaled, she said, "That was some goodbye fuck."

"Yeah. You could say that."

"What are you going to do?"

"Don't know. Go private."

Gloria chuckled and she turned to face him. "You, a private dick?"

Nash stared at her in the mirror on the opposite wall. It rested above a marked laminate benchtop. "I could always get a job with my brother-in-law as his gofer."

"Or you could come and work with us at the Federal Police," Gloria suggested.

"So you could screw me some more?"

She ran a finger over his hairy chest. "I admit, it would have its benefits."

"Nope. I'm done with it all. I want nothing to do with law enforcement from here on out. Nothing."

There was a drawn-out silence and all that could be heard was the tic-tic of the out-of-balance fan above them.

Gloria stubbed out her cigarette and said, "Oh, well. If you're sure?"

He wasn't. Being a cop was all he knew. "I am."

She swung out of bed and padded toward the shower. Nash watched the fluid way her muscles moved when she walked. The eagle tattoo across her shoulders stared back at him in all *its wondrous color.*

"You'll know where to find me if you change your mind,"
she said as she closed the door.

"Yeah," he murmured.

CHAPTER NINE

Gloria poked her head through the open door and said to Leroy, "My office, now."

"Here we go."

He walked into Gloria's office and stood in front of her desk She looked at him and asked, "Where are we at?"

"Not much further than yesterday, although we're reasonably sure that the bomb was placed in the car at the driver's home. He took it home on the same day every week to give it a detail."

"OK. Anybody see anything?"

"Nope. Not as far as we know. Annie has been trying to run down anyone who might have home security and CCTV vision for us, but not everyone is home."

"Bomb techs?"

"Still waiting."

Gloria thought for a moment. Then, "Have someone look into the driver's bank and phone records. Make sure that he's as squeaky clean as he seems. Someone might have paid him for access."

"Doing it as we speak."

"Good."

"Where's our undercover wonder?" Leroy asked smugly.

"He's not coming. So, I want you to tidy up any loose ends that you need to, and be ready to leave by tomorrow afternoon. I'll have Bellchambers ride shotgun. You'll have a foolproof back story by then and a file you'll need to memorize by the morning. Be prepared to be under for as long as it takes."

Leroy was confused. "You were going to send Nash out there on his own. Yet I get a babysitter. Why?"

"Because Nash is Nash and you are you. And I'm the boss so what I say goes. If you don't want to do it, I'll find somebody else."

"I didn't say that. I'll go."

"No, you won't," the voice from the doorway said. "All you'll do is get yourself killed. I'll go."

Dave Nash had arrived.

3:30 PM

There were four of them in Hoyland's office; Gloria, Leroy, Hoyland, and Nash. The boss stared at Nash and said, "You look like shit."

"I can do the job."

"I hope so because it's not just your arse on the line. Gloria went out on a limb for you."

Nash glanced at Gloria before returning his gaze to Hoyland. The commander continued, "Have you any idea what is required?"

"Nope."

Hoyland shot Gloria a questioning glance.

She moved away from the filing cabinet she had been leaning on and said, "You'll be going out to the northwest, to a town called Collari. It's on the Barwon River."

"I know where it is. I saw the report on TV."

"Good."

"What is it you want me to do? I gather it's tied up with the water situation?"

Gloria nodded. "You saw on the Four Corners' report about the inspectors who'd been threatened and such?"

"Yeah."

"About a week ago, one of them went missing. The police up there say they never even saw him. His name was Ray Petersen. The sergeant is saying he is looking into it."

"So why send me?"

"Because whatever is going on out there has to be tied in with the murder of Senator Worth. He was about to introduce a bill into the parliament to have all the big stations limited on water storage. It is a move that would have cost some of them millions. One, in particular, hundreds of millions."

"So, you think that whoever owns that one station, had the senator killed?"

"Yes."

"Well pull them in for questioning."

It was Hoyland who spoke next. "It isn't that simple. We need proof and we need to find out who owns it."

Nash raised his eyebrows. "You don't know?"

"No."

"Follow the money?"

"We tried that, but it is all funneled through shell companies until it is split through different banks around the globe. That's why we want you out there to find out what you can."

"What's my cover?"

Gloria hesitated. "Inspector for the water commission."

Nash laughed. "Shit. Didn't the last one disappear?"

"Yes. Which is why we think he must have found something."

"Am I on my own or will I have a backup?"

"You're on your own. If need be, we can have help to you in a couple of hours. You check in once a day. You miss it and we dispatch a team, so don't forget or you'll have half the AFP kicking down the door and your cover will be blown."

"Can I rely on local law enforcement?"

Hoyland said, "We don't know. This goes all the way back to Canberra. For all, we know, to the government itself. We'll set you up with all the kit you'll need."

"When do I leave?"

"Tomorrow. It'll take you a day to drive there."

"Am I AFP or PI?"

"You see this through, and I'll see about giving you a permanent job with this office."

"So, I'm a PI."

"A PI with powers and a gun. There's no way I would send one of my own out there unarmed. Anything else?"

"Nope. Not as yet."

"All right, I'll let Gloria deal with the finer details. After all, it's her op." Hoyland shifted his gaze to her. "Anything more about the bomb?"

Gloria shook her head. "We're still waiting on reports. The main thing that we're sure of is that the bomb was installed in the vehicle at the driver's home. We're doing a deep dive on him as we speak."

There was a knock on the door and Annie poked her head inside. "Sorry to interrupt, but I have footage of our suspect."

Hoyland nodded to Gloria. "Go. Check it out." He stood up and held out his right hand to Nash. "Good luck, Dave. Be careful out there."

4:15 PM

Nash watched over their shoulders as they all viewed the footage.

Annie said, by way of explanation, "It was attached to a house along the street and on the opposite side. The owners said that they'd been having trouble with kids knocking their bins over of a night, and they installed it to catch the little pricks. Their words, not mine."

The picture was black and white and dark. There was a street light, but it illuminated only part of the street and not the place where it was needed.

They ran through the vision until the time-stamp indicated **2:34 am**. At that time a car rolled slowly along the street and stopped two houses shy of the driver's.

It sat there in the dark for a couple of minutes before someone climbed out and crossed the street to disappear up the driveway.

When next the figure emerged, the timestamp read, **2:50 am.**

At no point was his, or her, face within sight.

"A fat lot of good that is," Leroy said. "We can't identify whoever it was from that."

"What about the car?" Nash suggested.

The vision was wound back far enough to place the vehicle directly under the streetlight, then they hit pause.

"What are you looking at, Dave?" Gloria asked.

"You see that the number plate is missing?"

"Yes."

"But there is damage to the rear bumper. You need to cross-reference that with any stolen vehicles, and see if anyone has made an insurance claim for something of that make and model."

"Anything else?" Leroy's voice was laced with sarcasm.

"Yes, there is," Nash's face grew hard. "Me staying alive depends on the rest of you doing your job properly. Don't fuck it up."

CHAPTER TEN

The man entered the office and stared at his boss. "I just got off the phone with one of our friends. An undercover is going to be sent up to Collari to sniff around."

His boss, dressed in a suit and tie, looked up from the paperwork he was working on. He stared at him with ice-blue eyes and asked, "Do you know who he is?"

"Apparently his name is Dave Nash."

"Seems to me I've heard that name before."

The man nodded. "Yeah. He took down some bikers a couple of years back. Then he quit the force."

"That's him. I remember now. The Outback Animals. They were a bad bunch."

"That's the guy."

The man behind the desk said, "Make a call. Let them know

he's coming. Give him a good old country welcome. If he turns out to be a problem, tell them to take care of him."

"OK."

"Now, what about the police investigation?"

"Our friend told me that the AFP have footage of the car and the driver."

"What? How?"

"CCTV from down the road."

The man behind the desk stood up and walked across to his office window. "Can they identify our guy?"

"No hope. Not in the dark."

"Good."

"There is one other thing," the man said to his boss.

"What is it?"

"There's a rumor going around that Romana could possibly submit the bill herself."

"We can't have that, can we? Send her a message. Let her know that we don't appreciate people who interfere where they're not wanted."

"Yes, sir. You want her out of the way?"

"No. Not yet. Let's try the softer approach."

"I'll take care of it."

CHAPTER ELEVEN

Gloria looked up from her clutter as Leroy came through the door. In his hand was a folder. He waved it around like a trophy. "I have the initial report from the bomb tech guys."

Gloria held out her hand. "Let's have a look."

She took the folder and opened it, selected the first sheet of paper and started to read. When she was finished, she said, "They haven't determined what kind of explosive was used, but the lack of physical evidence would indicate that a timer wasn't used."

"Which means that whoever detonated it had to be in the vicinity," Leroy observed.

Gloria nodded. "We need to widen the search area to see if we can find them. Traffic cameras, CCTV, private security, anything we can view and break down."

"It would be easier with more boots on the ground."

"I'll get them. In the meantime, go with what we've got."

8:45 AM

"I need some more bodies."

Hoyland glared at Gloria for the intrusion and said into the phone, "I'm sorry, sir, I'll have to call you back."

He replaced the receiver. "Good morning, sir. I would like some more bodies, please."

"I'm sorry, sir, but it can't wait."

"Obviously. What is it?"

"We need to widen our search. We've determined that the explosives were detonated from close by and not on a timer. So, I need more people to go door to door over a wider area to see if any of the homeowners might have home security vision we can use. Plus, we need to run down traffic cams and shop CCTV."

"I don't know, Gloria. We're pretty strapped for human resources right now."

"But, Pete, if he was close enough to hand detonate the bomb, we might catch a break. It was daylight, so I don't imagine that he would be sitting around for any length of time in a car with no number plates on it. We may have a better chance of tracking the car and finding out who it was."

"Our bomber doesn't seem to me to be careless enough to let his guard down that far."

"There's only one way to find out."

Hoyland raised his hands in surrender. "All right. I'll see what I can do. Let's hope you're right."

8:55 AM

Once Gloria was out in the hallway she reached into her pocket and took out her mobile. After punching in a number, she put it to her ear and waited.

"Hello?"

"We got more manpower, Annie. You coordinate them. Find me that bastard."

"Will do."

The line went dead.

CHAPTER TWELVE

Nash parked the Toyota Landcruiser with a boat in tow, outside the Collari pub and turned off the engine. He ran a hand through his hair and let out a long sigh. Glad to have arrived safely, what he wanted now more than anything was a beer and a feed. The pub would provide both.

Sitting in the cab of the 'Cruiser, he opened the glove compartment and looked at the .45 caliber Glock nestled in its holster next to the sat phone. He thought about stuffing it in his pants then dismissed the notion. He was in town. Surely he was safe enough there.

The Glock wasn't his only weapon. Gloria had supplied him with a Colt M4 carbine which was locked in a box, along with ammunition and tactical vest, in the back of the vehicle.

He slammed the glove box shut, locked it, and climbed out.

It was typical of a Friday night in a country pub, busy. The bar was packed with patrons as they washed away the week's work and caught up with friends. It was noisy and the jukebox was pumping out endless Creedence tracks. Cigarette smoke filled the air like a low, blue-grey mist. Obviously, the publican wasn't one to enforce the no-smoking laws.

Nash pushed his way through the crush and squeezed in between two men at the battered bar.

A tall, red-headed bargirl caught sight of him and called out as she pulled a couple of beers into frosty glasses, "Be with you in a minute, mate!"

Nash raised a hand to indicate he'd heard and looked around the bar while he waited. A few of the customers glanced in his direction but none seemed overly concerned or interested in the stranger in their midst.

He caught sight of a giant Murray Cod mounted on the back wall with a gold plaque underneath it. No doubt a tribute to the person who'd caught it. A large television screen hung on a wall in the far corner, broadcasting Friday Night Harness Racing on it and above it was a smaller screen with odds running across it.

"What can I get you, feller?" the bargirl asked.

Nash turned back to the bar. She gave him a broad smile which seemed to light up the freckles on her young face. His first reaction was, "How old are you?"

The smile never wavered. "Eighteen."

More like sixteen.

Nash opened his mouth to speak but was cut off by a different bargirl. One with a not so sunny disposition, and maybe six years older.

"Caroline, how many times do you have to be told, get the fuck out from behind the bar. Dad will kill you."

"Kerry…"

"Go."

The girl pouted and walked off. Kerry looked at Nash and said, "Sorry about that. She thinks she's helping but she's not. What can I get you?"

She had long black hair which was tied back and lacked the freckles on her tanned face that her sister had.

"I'd like a beer and a meal if possible? Is the kitchen still open?"

Kerry pointed at the board behind the bar. "Take your pick. I'll do your order after I get the beer. VB, Tooheys, or Carlton Draught?"

"A schooner of VB."

"Coming up."

He watched her walk along the bar to the beer taps, mesmerized by the way her butt-cheeks moved in the frayed, skintight denim shorts. A small amount of her back was exposed below her white singlet top, and Nash could see the markings of a tattoo.

"Forget it, buddy. You'll never get to sink your teeth into that arse."

Nash turned to stare at the man beside him. He wore a long-sleeved cotton shirt and an Akubra on his head. He was unshaven and Nash figured he'd be somewhere in his late twenties.

"Say what?" Nash asked.

"Just saw you looking. Thought I'd save you some problems. She's got a bloke who works out at Dawn Station."

Dawn Station.

"Tough crowd?"

"You have no idea."

Kerry came back with his beer and placed it on the bar. "Four bucks."

Nash put a twenty dollar note on the bar and Kerry took it. She paused and asked, "Passing through? Tourist?"

"Water inspector."

Her face fell. "Oh. Sad about that other feller who went missing."

"Yeah. You know him?"

"Not really. Came in here for a meal once or twice. Sad that he drowned out there on the river."

"He drowned? I thought he was still missing?"

"That's the rumor. They found his boat and all, but not him."

"Kerry! Get us another beer, love?" a customer called from along the bar.

She gave him a wave. To Nash, she said, "You figure out what you want to eat?"

He glanced at the board and ordered the one thing that stuck out. "I'll have the steak and chips, please."

Kerry reached to her left and grabbed an order book. She

scribbled down his order and asked, "How do you have it, and do you want gravy on that?"

"Medium, and hold the gravy. You've got Dead Horse, I take it?"

"Yeah. One steak, chips and sauce coming up. Medium rare."

8:50 PM

Nash noticed them come in as he was forking the last of the chips into his mouth. The door opened and three men entered, a swagger to their step.

From where he sat at the table, he watched them cross the floor towards the bar. All wore jeans and shirts with the sleeves ripped from them, and Akubras. Nash immediately knew that they weren't who they pretended to be. Their tattoos gave that away.

Even at the distance, he was from them, he could see that these men were ex-military. The way they carried themselves suggested either SAS or Commandos. He'd seen men like these before. Police special operations were full of them.

They were greeted at the bar by Kerry who leaned forward for a lingering kiss between herself and the man with the red shirt. She seemed excited, and the pair swapped words as she served them.

Then he looked in Nash's direction and Nash got a distinct impression that trouble was about to start.

Kerry left them to serve other customers and her boyfriend pushed away from the bar and pointed himself in Nash's direction. His friends followed.

They weaved their way between customers and tables and stopped in front of the PI. Nash studied them with a practiced eye. The boyfriend and his mates were all around the same height, six-one, maybe six-two. All were unshaven and very well built.

Nash took a sip from his beer and asked, "Something I can help you blokes with?"

"Kerry said you're the new water inspector feller up from the city," her boyfriend said. "Is that right?"

"Who are you?"

"Ringa."

Nash nodded. "Yes, that's right. I've come to look over the pumps along the river."

"You won't need to check on Dawn Station's. Our pumps are fine."

Nash raised his eyebrows. "Really? That's good to hear. I guess I'll see for myself when I check them."

The deadpan expression on Ringa's face never wavered. He said, "You obviously didn't hear me. I said they were fine."

"Uh-huh. You sound like you don't want me to do my job."

"We got nothing against you doing your job, just against trespassers. And to check the pumps, you'll have to trespass on Dawn Station. We got signs up about trespassers. They get shot."

Nash nodded. "I'd hate to trespass on someone's property.

Thanks for the advice."

Ringa leaned forward and placed his palms flat on the tabletop. When he spoke, his voice was low with more than just a hint of menace. "Be careful on that river, Nash. Accidents can happen out there."

Shit! They knew his name. Which meant they knew that he was coming. But worst of all, the AFP had a damned leak.

Nash remained silent and Ringa pushed away from the table. "As I said, be careful. Wouldn't want something to happen to you like the last bloke."

They turned and walked back toward the bar.

Nash finished his beer and got up from his table. He approached the bar and signaled to Kerry, all the while under the watchful eye of the three Dawn Station men.

"Would you like another beer?" she asked.

Nash shook his head. "You got a room I can use?"

"Sure, I'll get you a key."

She returned with the key and handed it to him. "Rooms are seventy a night, but fix me up in the morning when it's a little less busy. Pay for the meal then too."

He shrugged. "OK."

Kerry gave him a warm smile and said, "It's all good. See you then."

He turned away from the bar and found one of Ringa's mates standing there blocking his path.

So this is how it was going to be. A pissing contest to see if he was capable.

The PI smiled. "Sorry, cobber. Didn't see you there."

The man stood with his feet apart, arms folded, and staring through beady eyes. His nose had been broken at least once, and through the stubble on his face, Nash could make out a thin scar.

Suddenly the room grew quiet with anticipation.

"Ringa, stop this," Kerry called out.

"I ain't Jacko's father. You know how he gets when he takes a dislike to someone."

"There's nothing wrong with him. He's just a damned water inspector."

Ringa shrugged.

Kerry came from behind the bar and placed herself between the two men. "This stops here," she hissed.

Nash held up his hands. "All I want to do is get my gear from my car and head off to my room."

Kerry pleaded with her boyfriend again, "Ringa?"

"I wouldn't stand there, babe. You're likely to get hurt."

She gave Nash a sorrowful look, who said, "He's probably right. I'll be fine."

Her expression was doubtful but she moved back behind the bar. Once she was out of the firing line, Nash took off his coat and revealed tattooed arms ripped with cords of muscle.

Jacko glanced at them and Nash smiled. "You aren't the only tough guy. I've got some too."

"Huh?"

Then Nash hit him.

His right fist flashed forward and struck Jacko in the throat. The bully was stunned and took a step back. Nash followed and hit him again, this time flush on the nose. He felt it give under his fist and blood gushed forth from the broken extremity. But Jacko remained on his feet.

It was the third blow that was the killer. Nash noticed the spread of the bully's feet and stepped in closer. He brought his right boot up and kicked him in the crotch.

With a howl of pain, Jacko fell to his knees, his bloody face turning purple. Around him, Nash heard the crowd give a sickening groan. He was about to hit him again when he changed his mind and pushed the stricken man to one side.

With a groan, Jacko hit the floor and hunched over as pain ripped through him.

The PI turned to face Ringa. "You find out what you wanted to?"

"Yeah," he growled. "I guess I did. Not bad for a water inspector."

Nash picked up his coat. "This water inspector has been around a bit."

"So it would seem."

Jacko moaned and the PI said, "You might want to get him checked out."

"I'll do that."

"See you around."

"Yeah, count on it."

Ringa watched him walk towards the door. This bloke was going to be trouble.

CHAPTER THIRTEEN

CANBERRA
FRIDAY, 9:32 PM

The phone next to her bed rang and Gloria picked it up. "Browning."

"The bastards know."

"Nash? What do you mean?"

"Dawn Station. They knew I was coming, and they know who I fucking am. They sent some blokes to look me over."

"Shit!" Gloria exclaimed then glanced to her right at the small bundle asleep beside her.

"Exactly."

"That means we have a damn leak in the AFP."

"It does."

"Damn it, I'm pulling you out," she snapped. "Come tomorrow you get in your car and get back here. You're done. Crap, Hoyland's going to have a field day when I tell him."

"No," Nash said.

"What do you mean no?"

"Don't tell Hoyland. Find the damned leak. You can trust no one. Except maybe your team."

"You sound like you're not coming in."

"That's right. They've shown their hand so I'm going to see it through."

"But they know you're working for the AFP."

"Makes it more interesting, doesn't it?"

"Let me send someone to help you, then," Gloria suggested. "Leroy."

"No, I'm fine."

"All right, but be careful."

"You know me. I can take care of myself."

CANBERRA
11:15 PM

Gloria fumbled with the phone and cursed it in her drowsy state. She looked at the clock beside the bed and saw it was quarter-past eleven. "Christ, this better be good."

"Yes?" it was abrupt and straight to the point.

"We got him!"

Annie!

"Say again?"

"We have footage of the car that the bomber used, a white '09 Ford Falcon. It's registered to a man named Michael Flaherty. He's in the system for firearms offenses. He lives in Canberra and we have cars on the way to pick him up now."

"Great work, Annie. I'll be in shortly."

"We've got this, boss. Stay there. Come in the morning."

"No. I'm coming now."

Gloria disconnected and then rang another number. When the person on the other end answered, she said, "I'm sorry to do this, but I need you."

SATURDAY
12:30 AM

Leroy and Annie were in the conference room when Gloria arrived. However, as soon as she entered, she sensed that there was an issue.

Tossing her bag on the table, she said, "Talk to me. Where are we at?"

"He was gone," Leroy informed her. "The house was empty, and his car wasn't there either."

Gloria's heart sank. "Damn it. Was there anything in the house?"

Annie said, "Crime scene is still going over it. But initially, they found some wires and other electronic stuff."

"So, he's definitely our guy?"

"Looks that way."

"Right, turn his life upside down. I want him found. I'll let Hoyland know."

1:06 AM

A phone rang.

The man answered. "Yes?"

"They found your man. He got careless and used his own car. The AFP raided his place but he wasn't there."

The man sat up in his bed. "It was a damn good thing he wasn't. What the hell do I pay you for? It should never have got that far."

"I'm telling you now."

The man hung up. "Shit!"

CHAPTER FOURTEEN

The phone in his pocket rang.

"Yes?"

"We have a problem with our friend. He got careless and now the AFP are all over his house."

The man looked at Flaherty who was staring out the window and across the street towards their target. "What do you want me to do?"

"Make the problem go away."

He hung up and replaced the phone in his pocket. Flaherty asked, "Is everything OK?"

"Yeah, it's fine," the man lied. "Get your gear. It's time."

The air outside was cool. They crossed the road and the man asked Flaherty, "Are you sure there is no CCTV in the office?"

"Yep."

"What about the alarm?"

"It won't matter, will it? We break in, set the bomb to detonate in a couple of minutes, and then we get the hell out. Security won't even be halfway here by the time our tail lights disappear around the corner."

The office was small. Probably because the senator was hardly ever there. Her secretary was the person who spent all her time there, relaying messages to her boss wherever she happened to be at the time; most of which were never replied to.

Flaherty knelt and worked quickly on the device. It was set to go off within two minutes. Holding up a mobile phone, he said, "All I have to do is hit speed dial and boom."

"Good," said the man who took out his gun and shot Flaherty in the head. Relieving him of the phone, he exited the office.

The man set off walking along the footpath and made a call. "I need you to pick me up from Goulburn."

A few more words were exchanged and then he hung up. Next, he hit the speed dial button.

CANBERRA
2:02 AM

Gloria was in her office when the call came through. Leroy poked his head around the corner and said, "You aren't going to believe this."

"What?"

"Someone just blew up Senator Romana Fielding's office in Goulburn."

Gloria slumped back in her chair. "Bloody hell. Was there anybody hurt?"

Leroy shrugged. "Not sure yet. They're still putting out the fire."

"Too much of a coincidence, isn't it?"

"Let's see. First, her piece of nooky gets himself blown up. Then she announces that she's going to push ahead with the water bill and her office goes the same way. Yeah, I think so."

Gloria remained thoughtful for a moment and then said, "It has to be a warning. I mean, she's hardly ever there. My guess is that's why they picked it."

Suddenly Annie appeared, a broad smile on her face. "Come and have a look at this."

Gloria and Leroy frowned at each other and followed Annie out into one of the conference rooms. There they found her standing in front of a television screen, watching ABC's News 24 channel.

It was showing a recurrent feed of firemen fighting a large fire in Goulburn. Orange flames leaped into the air while the firemen had two hoses trying to douse the flames. Every now and then the camera would pan away.

Along the bottom of the screen was a news ticker with the words, *Breaking News: A bomb blast has rocked central Goulburn*.

"There!" Annie said as the camera panned once more.

Gloria stepped forward. "What am I looking at?"

"Are you perving on hunky firemen again, Annie?" Leroy quipped.

"Shut up. Wait."

They all waited patiently for a further three minutes and when Annie found what she was looking for, she hit the PAUSE LIVE TV button on the remote she held. "There."

They stared at the screen in silence. No one said a word for a long, drawn-out time. Then Gloria said, "It is it, isn't it?"

"Looks that way," Leroy agreed.

"Damn right it is," Annie said. "It's the bloody car we're looking for."

Gloria whirled about and called over her shoulder as she headed for the door, "Come on, Annie."

"Where are we going?"

"Goulburn. Leroy, get in contact with whoever is in charge up there and fill them in on that car."

GOULBURN
3:30 AM

When Gloria and Annie arrived, the fire had been extinguished and road-blocks set up in a one-block radius. They flashed their badges and were let through by a young constable. Gloria said to Annie, "I'll have a chat with the man in charge. I want you to look around and see what you can find out."

Annie reached into her pocket and took out a pair of latex gloves. She put them on and then walked across to Flaherty's car. There was a constable standing beside it and she asked him, "Has anyone touched this?"

"No, ma'am. Not since the call came through."

"Thanks."

She opened the passenger side door and looked inside. It was dark and smelled like body odor. Standing up straight, she called across to the constable. "You got a torch on you?"

He smiled at her. "Sure."

When he didn't move, Annie sighed. "Can I borrow it?"

"Oh, sure."

He fumbled with it and walked around the car to give it to her. "Here you are, sorry."

She flicked the light on and then shone it into the car. The front was relatively tidy, apart from the usual dirt and grime on the floor from not having seen a vacuum for some time. The seat covers were old and worn too. The back seat, however, was a different story. Obviously, the guy was a fast-food junkie. Bulging paper bags from McDonald's, plastic ones from KFC, pie wrappers, and empty Coke cans were tossed everywhere. The vehicle was a rubbish tip on wheels.

Annie screwed up her nose and flicked open the glove compartment. It fell open and she rifled through the paper-work it contained. Removing something that looked to be a bill, she shone the torch on it. The name at the top read: *Michael Flaherty*.

"Bingo."

Straightening up, she said to the constable, "Get a tow truck here and have this car transported back to Canberra."

He seemed about to protest when a call from over the road distracted them both. "I've got a body here."

Annie stared and saw a fireman standing on top of some smoldering ruins. She hurried across the street and was met there by Gloria who'd heard the shout too.

"It's him," Annie said definitively.

"What makes you say that?"

"The car across the road is his. If he was still alive, then it wouldn't be."

Gloria nodded. "Makes sense, I guess. Maybe he stuffed up."

"Maybe. What did the boss man have to say?"

"Nothing much. The explosion occurred around one-thirty, and so far, nobody saw a thing. I guess it'll all come out with forensics."

"What about CCTV?"

"I'm not too sure about the other businesses. Looks like it'll be down to good old police work to find out."

Annie grimaced. "I guess we'd best get started then."

CHAPTER FIFTEEN

GOULBURN
SATURDAY, 6:30 AM

Gloria stared across the road as crime scene techs began sifting through the charred rubble of the office. Annie came across to her and said, "They'll move the body out soon and ship it to Canberra where our medical examiner can do their thing."

Gloria ran a hand through her hair, suddenly exhausted. "I could use a shower and some sleep."

"You and me both. I rang the office and forensics are waiting ready to receive the car."

"Good. Did you have any luck finding us a witness?"

"Nope."

"Shit!"

Gloria's phone buzzed in her pocket. She took it out and looked at the illuminated screen. It was Leroy. She pressed the accept button and put it up to her ear and gave a tired, "Yeah?"

"How goes it, Boss?"

"Slowly. Is that car back yet?"

"Nope."

"What do you want?"

"I have something of interest for you," Leroy said.

"OK, what?"

"Our man Flaherty did some work with our friendly neighborhood water minister back in twenty-fourteen. On his property out in Orange."

Gloria nodded. "Just wait while I put you on speaker."

"OK."

Gloria stared at the phone as though in a trance. "Fuck, where is it?"

Annie leaned in and touched the screen. "There."

With a snort of disgust, she mumbled something and then said, "Thanks. All right, Leroy, speak."

"So, like I said, in twenty-fourteen, our boy Flaherty worked for Tom Whitfield."

Annie's eyes lit up. She had to control herself before she blurted it out. She managed to say quietly, "The water minister?"

"That's him," Leroy confirmed.

Annie noticed the expression change on her boss' face. "You just had a thought?"

"Uh-huh. Back in twenty-fourteen, I recall a bomb going off out in Orange. A couple of people were killed."

"Very interesting," said Leroy.

"Indeed. Leroy, find out what you can about it. Have it done by the time we get back."

"Will do, boss," he said and hung up.

Gloria put the phone back in her pocket and stared at Annie. "Go and check how much longer they're going to be before they get that body out of there. I need it back in Canberra so we can try to get a positive ID."

"What if it isn't our man?"

Gloria shivered and for the first time that morning felt the cold chill in the air. "I don't want to think about it."

COLLARI
7:30 AM

Dave Nash had just returned from having a shower in the communal bathroom at the end of the hall when knuckles rapped loudly on the door. With only a towel wrapped around him, Nash's first instinct was to grab the Glock from under his pillow.

The knock came again, this time louder.

"Who is it?" Nash called out.

"Collari Police."

"Christ," Nash cursed and placed the weapon back under the pillow.

He crossed the thin-carpeted floor and unlocked the door. Then he turned the handle and swung it open. In the dim hall of the pub stood a middle-aged, uniformed policeman with a mustache.

"Are you Nash?" he asked.

"Word gets around," Nash said.

"Small town."

"Uh-huh. What can I do for you …?"

"Sergeant Chris Royall."

"What can I do for you, Sergeant Royall?" Nash asked.

"Can I come in?"

Nash stepped back from the doorway. "Be my guest."

Royall moved across the threshold and into the small room. Looking around, he turned back to face Nash who had just closed the door.

"I heard you had some trouble last night," the sergeant started.

"Nothing I couldn't handle."

Royall walked over to the window and stared out through the curtain. A battered old Toyota Landcruiser with a hole in its exhaust roared past, doing its best to wake the town. When he turned back, the expression on his lined face had changed.

"Why the fuck is there a Federal copper in my town without me knowing about it?" he snarled.

And there it was.

"I'm not a Federal Policeman," Nash told said truthfully.

"Bullshit. You work for them."

Nash nodded. "I do."

"What happened to fucking professional courtesy?" Royall barked. "I should have been the first place you stopped when you hit town. Not the pub."

Nash shrugged.

"Well, why are you here?"

"I'm on holiday?"

"Fuck off!"

"You tell me," Nash said. "Everybody knows who I am. Why don't you all know why?"

"Well, since you're meant to be posing as a water inspector, I'd say that it would have something to do with the last guy's disappearance?"

Nash had a feeling he knew more than he was letting on. "Let's just say it has to do with the water and leave it at that."

Royall nodded abruptly. "Fine. But let me tell you this. Collari is my town. You don't get to come up here and upset all the locals. Stick to your investigation and stay out of things that don't concern you. Got it?"

"Yeah, I guess I do. Now, what can you tell me about the feller who disappeared?"

"Fuck you, arsehole," Royall swore at him and stormed out of the room.

Nash closed the door and walked over to the bedside table and picked up his phone. He dialed in Gloria's number and then put it to his ear.

"Hello?"

"It's me," he said.

"Are you OK?" There was concern in her voice.

"Yeah, I'm fine. I'm just checking in. How about you?"

Gloria told him about the bomb and the body. She also filled him in on how the chief suspect had worked for Tom Whitfield.

Once she was finished, Nash said, "Could you run a check on a couple of people for me?"

"Sure, just give me their names."

"First person is called Ringa. I guess it's spelled how it sounds. Cross-reference it against a military background. Maybe special forces."

"Sure, no problems," Gloria told him. "I can do it when we get back. Who's the second."

"Police Sergeant Chris Royall. He heads up the station here. I just had a visit from him, and he wasn't very happy. There's something off about him."

"You think he's bent?"

"I don't know. He seemed to know a lot about me, but that might be like he said, small town. I'd like to make sure though."

"OK, I'll see what I can find out. Anything else?"

"Nope, that's about all. I'll check in tonight. I'm headed out on the river to look around."

"Dave?"

"Yeah."

"Be careful out there."

"You know me, Gloria. I'm always careful."

CHAPTER SIXTEEN

Leroy met them at the doors of the elevator. "It's about time you two got back. I did that digging you wanted and came up with gold."

Gloria said, "Talk while we walk. If I stop, I'll fall down."

"It turns out that Flaherty was working on the Whitfield property when that bomb went off," Leroy said. He held up a file in his hand. "I had this emailed through. It's everything they had on it."

Gloria took it and opened it. By the time she reached her office, she'd flicked through most of it. "Says here that they arrested someone for it."

"Yep, he's doing life in Goulburn. The bomb killed two of Whitfield's business associates. The feller who confessed to the bomb was a third."

Gloria placed the file down on top of the mess on her desk. "He confessed?"

"Sure did. The whole case was open and shut."

"But why did he do it?" Annie asked. "Why did he confess?"

Leroy shrugged.

"OK, leave the file with me. Both of you go home and get some rest. We'll get back to this on Monday morning. Besides, we won't have much until then. We're just waiting to see if the body is who we think it is before we conduct our next move."

"Are you sure?" Leroy asked.

"That's where I'm going, right after I do a couple of things."

COLLARI
9:52 AM

There was one other car and trailer at the Collari boat ramp when Nash went to put his tinny in the water. It was a beat-up old mid-eighties Holden Commodore with more dents than a car after a Saturday night demolition derby.

It was a rust color, most of which Nash thought was red dirt because between the streaks he could make out a darker green. It also had a sticker on the back which read: *Aussie Farmers Doing It Tough!*

"Not wrong there, mate," Nash murmured.

He backed the trailer down the boat ramp and put the boat in the water. Parking his vehicle, he got out and locked it up, thinking long and hard about taking the M4 but dismissed it.

He still had the Glock, so it would have to do.

Five minutes later he was in the dinghy and traveling downriver.

CANBERRA
10:15 AM

"Hello?"

"Is that you, Mack?"

"Gloria?" Mack McKenzie asked, surprised.

"The one and only."

"It's been a while. What can I do for you?"

"I need your help with something I'm working on," she told him.

"If you're ringing New South Wales Internal Affairs, it must be serious."

"My team and I are working on this thing down here in Canberra and ..."

"You got the bombing of that Senator?"

"Yes."

There was silence on the end of the line.

"Are you there, Mack?"

"Yes. Before we go any further, do you want this call recorded?"

Gloria thought about it for a moment and then said, "Yes. Just in case."

"Wait a second then."

There was a pause for longer than a second before he came back and said, "All right. Let's go."

"What can you tell me about a police sergeant by the name of Chris Royall?"

"Christ," Mack said. "That's a name I haven't heard in a while. Why?"

"I have an undercover … sorry, he was an undercover but apparently this office leaks like a fucking sieve. Anyway, his name came up in the town of Collari."

"Are you saying your UC's cover is blown and he's still out there?" Mack asked, bewildered.

"I tried to pull him in, but he wouldn't come."

"What does a bombing in Canberra have to do with a police sergeant in Collari?" the Internal Affairs officer asked.

"Dave Nash …"

"Wait," Mack snapped, cutting her off. "You have Dave Nash as a UC in the field?"

Gloria hesitated. "Yes."

Mack almost came through the phone. "For fuck's sake, Gloria. That prick is unhinged. Why the hell would the Feds even have him on their books?"

"Because he's good at what he does, Mack," Gloria pointed out. "And at this point in time, his arse is hanging out to dry with no backup."

"Shit, this just gets better."

"Dave is looking into the disappearance of a water inspector in that area. Which we think is linked to the death of the senator who was trying to push through new laws," Gloria explained, leaving out the bit about Whitfield.

"Wait a minute. There was an explosion in Goulburn overnight. Is there something in that one as well? Wasn't it some other senator's office?"

"Yes. Romana Fielding. She and Worth were screwing. We had a lead on the bomber and raided his home, but he wasn't there. But we think he was killed in the Goulburn explosion. I'm waiting on test results."

"Case closed then," Mack observed.

"Not by a longshot. Chris Royall, Mack?"

"Yes, right. Royall is an outcast. He was posted out to Collari because the higherups thought he was bent. We investigated him but couldn't come up with anything concrete."

"So, he was reassigned?"

"That's about it."

"Who was he on the take from?"

"He was posted out of Orange. There was some mob activity happening there at the time and he was accused of taking kickbacks."

Gloria sat forward in her chair, her grip tightening on the phone. "Did you say Orange?"

"Sure did."

"Was he there in twenty-fourteen about the time of the bombing?"

"Give me a minute."

In the background, Gloria could hear fingers tapping on a keyboard. Then Mack's voice came back over the phone. "Says here he was transferred soon after that to Collari."

"Shit."

"I take it that it means something?" Mack asked.

"Possibly. Do you still have contacts in the ADF?"

"Sure."

"If I give you another name, could you check it out. Dave is sure that the man served at one time or another."

There was a moment of silence followed by a crash. Then, "Fuck it. Give me the name and I'll write it down after I get off the phone."

"It's Ringa."

"Is that it?"

"That's all Dave gave me."

Mack sighed. "All right, I'll see what I can come up with. Just don't expect to hear back from me before Monday."

"I won't. Thanks, Mack."

"Watch your arse, Gloria. It sounds like this could be something big."

Gloria hung up and stared at the notes she'd been making on the note pad. Then she drew a circle around the name Chris Royall. So that made two suspicious people who were in Orange at the time of the bombing there.

Flaherty worked for Whitfield, and Royall was on the take. Maybe from Whitfield? It was possible. Gloria reached out and picked up the phone again. She dialed in the numbers and waited for the call to be answered.

"Hello?"

"Leroy? What were the names of those associates who were killed in twenty-fourteen?"

"Not sure off the top of my head. The file is locked in my desk. Do you want me to come back in and dig them out?"

"No, it's fine. Just have them on my desk first thing Monday before I head on up to Goulburn."

"Sure. I'll take care of it."

Gloria hung up and then dialed a second number. The voice on the phone told her it couldn't be connected so she hung up. Looking at her watch she thought, *stuff it, time to go home and spend some time with Rachel.*

CHAPTER SEVENTEEN

Nash looked at his map and then at the two centrifugal pumps ahead of him. Each had the capacity to pump one-hundred and sixty megalitres of murky brown water per day. All were working. He edged the dinghy over to the riverbank and stepped out. Reaching around behind his back, he felt for the Glock. It was still tucked in the waistband.

Nash started towards the top of the bank with slow steps. In each direction, long lines of Rivergums stretched out as far as the eye could see. In the treetops a crow cawed, protesting the intruder's presence. It was immediately answered by the squawk of a Sulphur Crested Cockatoo.

Reaching the top of the bank, Nash paused to look at the vista. The Rivergums stopped no more than fifty meters beyond where he stood, giving way to a vast expanse of nothingness; a barren landscape seemingly devoid of life.

He glanced to his left and stared at the pumps which spewed forth over thirteen million liters of water per hour with awesome force into an irrigation ditch that cut through the paddock towards a large earthen wall in the distance.

Looking at the map again, Nash read the words: **Piccadilly Station**.

Beside the irrigation ditch was a shed that housed the pump motors. Above it was a security camera. Nash walked over to the shed and opened the door. The pumps roared with life. Looking around, he found a box and shrugged. He guessed it might be the meter box, but what would he know?

Nash opened it and found what he wanted. It seemed to be working fine.

Suddenly, the approaching roar of a vehicle could be heard. Nash closed the box and walked out of the pump shed. He closed the door and turned to watch the white Landcruiser with tray back bouncing towards him.

The four-wheel-drive lurched to a stop and a grey-haired man in his sixties, wearing jeans and cotton shirt climbed from it. Ramming a stained Akubra on his head he gave Nash a shitty stare and snapped, "Who the fuck are you?"

"Dave Nash, new water inspector."

"You got any identification?"

"Sure," Nash said, patting at his pockets. "Must have left it in the dinghy. Who are you?"

"Mike Reilly. I own Piccadilly Station. You the feller they sent after the last one disappeared?"

"Yes."

"Mighty strange if you ask me," Reilly said. "Man just disappearing like that."

"You got any idea why he might have disappeared?" Nash asked.

"Is this your first time out here?"

Nash nodded. "Yes. Are you going to make me walk back to the boat to get my identification?"

Reilly shook his head. "No."

"So, do you?"

"Do I what?"

"Have any idea why a man might disappear out here?"

Reilly looked at him thoughtfully and asked, "Feel like a ride?"

Nash frowned. "Where we going?"

"Not far."

"OK."

"Come on," Reilly said and started walking towards the Landcruiser.

Nash followed him and noted the puffs of dust raised with each step. It sure was a parched country.

They climbed in the vehicle and straight away Nash noted the intense heat of no air-conditioning. Reilly started the vehicle and shoved it into gear. It leaped forward and lurched over a deep rut. The station owner said, "By the way, did you find anything wrong with my meters?"

"No, they looked fine."

"And so they should. Unlike some others around here."

"How do you mean?"

Reilly let the question go through and Nash didn't push it. "What do you farm?"

"Cotton."

"Take a fair amount of water?"

Reilly nodded. "Thirsty bastard stuff, cotton. If you don't have the water to start with, you won't make it in the business."

The Landcruiser came to a stop before a large embankment which Nash guessed was around thirteen feet high. "We're here," Reilly said and climbed out.

Nash followed him and they ascended the earthen wall. The sight before them was astounding.

"You asked why a man might disappear out here, Nash," Reilly said. "Well, there it is. Water."

It was awesome to see. Enough water to fill a small harbor.

"Holy shit," Nash muttered.

"I have another two the same size. It is the lifeblood of the land. And some men can't get enough of it."

"How much water is there?" Nash asked.

"In liters or dollars?"

"Either?"

"If I was to sell some of it, I could make upwards of seventy million dollars. And I'm not the biggest hoarder of the stuff. Now, imagine what they are sitting on, and then work out how much money it is worth."

"What about Dawn Station?" Nash asked.

Reilly's face changed and he turned away. "Come on, let's get you back to your little ship."

Again, Nash let it go and followed him down the bank

towards the Landcruiser. They climbed back in and he asked Reilly, "What is the next station along the river?"

"Dawn Station."

"How far?"

"You don't want to be going there, Nash. My advice is to stay away."

"I've got a job to do."

Reilly snorted. "You're no more a water inspector than I am."

"Is it that obvious?"

"When you've seen as many of them as I have, then yes, it is. So, who are you?"

"I work for the AFP. I'm out here investigating the disappearance of the previous water inspector."

"And you figure that it has something to do with Dawn Station? Is that it?"

"In a fashion."

"Uh-huh. That doesn't surprise me."

"What else can you tell me?"

There was a drawn-out silence before Reilly said, "I'm going to town after I've finished here. Got to meet a man at the pub. How about we have a meal and I'll tell you all I know."

"Are you sure you want to be seen with me? They already know I'm a UC. Someone warned them I was coming."

Reilly chuckled. "Nah, I'm too old to be worried about them. Sounds like you've got more troubles than me."

Nash said, "I'll meet you there about eight? Maybe I should know more about my enemy before I go shitting in his back yard."

"Son, if they catch you, they'll make you eat it."

CHAPTER EIGHTEEN

COLLARI
5:06 PM

Nash had just finished loading the dinghy onto the boat trailer when his phone rang. "Yeah?"

"You're a hard man to track down, Mr. Nash," Gloria said.

"I've been out on the river most of the day."

"Learn anything?"

"A little. I'm having dinner tonight with a station owner who might be able to answer some of my questions. How about you?"

"I have a dinner date with the most gorgeous girl in the whole world."

"Rachel?"

"Yes, Rachel."

There was a noise in the background and Gloria said, "She says hello."

Nash felt his mouth open but the words he wanted to utter the most refused to come out. Instead, there was silence. Gloria's voice came through the phone, "Are you still there?"

"I'm here. What did you find out today?"

"I talked to an officer I know in Internal Affairs …"

"Not fucking Mack McKenzie?"

"Yes, it was, in fact," she answered. "I'm thinking there is something between you two."

"He tried for years to nail me on stuff because I screwed his wife."

"You what?"

"Don't judge me before you know the facts," Nash told her. "For starters, I didn't know who she was or even that she was married. I didn't even know she was Mack's wife until he walked in on us."

"No wonder he has a hard-on for you."

"That's a picture I could do without. Continue," he said.

"He told me that your friend, Royall was suspected of being on the take. He was transferred out there after they couldn't pin anything on him."

"That doesn't surprise me," Nash said. "I just get that feeling about him. What else?"

"This is where it gets interesting. Royall came from Orange and was there when a car-bomb went off, killing two men on Whitfield's property. He was transferred shortly after. Now, our bombmaker, Flaherty, worked for Whitfield at the time the bomb went off. Another man confessed to it and is now doing life in Goulburn prison."

"Who were the ones that were killed?" Nash asked.

"I'm not sure at this time. I haven't got the file, but I'll have the information on Monday. I'm also going to take a drive to Goulburn prison to interview the supposed killer."

"Any news on the leak front?" he asked Gloria.

"Nothing as yet."

"I'd better go," Nash said. "I'll check in tomorrow."

"You be careful, Dave," Gloria told him.

"Can't be careful and catch bad guys, Gloria."

"Dave ..."

"Tell me something," he said, cutting her off.

"What?"

"Does she look like you?"

Gloria went quiet and he thought he'd gone too far. Then Gloria said in a soft voice, "Yes, a little. But mostly like her father."

Then she hung up.

Nash stared at the phone in his hand. A million thoughts ran through his head. The foremost was one that he'd asked so many times since he'd found out that Gloria had a child. Was she his?

COLLARI PUB
7:54 PM

Saturday night and the bar in the Collari pub was packed. Nash squeezed through gaps in the crowd and finally made it to the bar.

He caught sight of Kerry and gave her a wave. She looked at him and then went back to pulling a beer to fill an order. Her expression was completely different from the one the night before.

Then he saw Caroline serving as well. She spotted him and came along the bar. "Hiya, cowboy, what can I get you?"

"Schooner of VB will do, thanks."

She went away to the taps and filled a frosty glass. When she came back, the drink was placed on the beer mat which absorbed the froth running down the side. He paid for the drink and said, "What's up with your sister?"

Caroline looked at her and then back to Nash. "Boyfriend troubles."

"Ringa?"

"Arsehole more like it."

Nash let it go. Instead, he asked, "Have you seen Reilly from Piccadilly Station in here?"

She nodded. "Saw him earlier. I think he was in the lounge."

Nash raised his eyebrows in mock surprise. "You guys have a lounge?"

"Of course." she stopped when she realized that he was having her on. "Good on ya. It's through there."

Caroline was pointing to a door to his right. He smiled at her. "Thanks. And you really shouldn't be behind there."

She smiled back. "Are you a cop or something?"

It seemed that everybody knew.

"Caroline!" Kerry shouted along the bar. "Move your arse!"

Nash stared at her and saw the angry expression on her

face. But that wasn't all he saw. In spite of all the makeup she wore, it couldn't hide the tell-tale bruise around her right eye. It looked like Ringa had been busy.

Nash walked through the crowd and opened the door to the lounge. Stepping through, he stopped just inside. There was wood-paneling around the walls of the dimly lit room and a flat-screen television on the wall, Keno numbers flashing upon it.

Like the bar, the place was busy, and the sound of cutlery on plates came frequently. Over in a dark corner, he saw a man sitting alone sucking on a cigarette. "Obviously the no-smoking policy hasn't reached this far west yet," Nash murmured.

Then he saw Reilly. The station owner was sitting at a table, talking to another man. Nash approached them and they looked up at him.

"I see you made it," Reilly said.

"I don't mind a good pub feed."

"This is ..." Reilly started, but before he could finish, the other man cut him off.

"I'm leaving," the man said and stood up then walked away without another word.

"Something I said?" Nash asked.

"The times we live in, I'm afraid."

Nash sat down and picked up a menu. "What won't kill you on this thing?"

"Surprisingly, most of the food is good. I try to get into town of a Saturday night to catch up with friends."

"Was old mate one?"

"Larry? Sure. I've known him for years."

"Station owner?"

Reilly gave Nash an even stare. "Shall we order?"

"Why not?"

Twenty minutes later, Kerry arrived carrying their meals and cutlery wrapped in serviettes. She avoided Nash's stare and walked away.

"Waste of a promising future that one," Reilly observed.

The PI cut his pepper steak, and said, "How so?"

"She could have been anything. Very smart. Top of her class in school. But then her mother died and her damned father roped her into working here and that was that."

"What about the other sister, Caroline?"

"She never stood a chance."

They kept eating their meals. Nash placed his cutlery on the plate and pushed it away from him. He sipped his beer and then waited for Reilly. When the station owner was finished with his, he asked, "What can you tell me about Dawn Station?"

Reilly wiped his mouth on his napkin and said, "What do you want to know?"

"Whatever you can tell me?"

"How long do you have?"

Nash took another sip from his beer. "I've got all night."

CHAPTER NINETEEN

Caroline put another VB schooner on the table and placed a glass of light beer in front of Reilly. Nash waited until she was gone and asked, "What do you think happened to the previous water guy?"

"Ray Petersen?"

"You knew him?"

"Sure. He was a nice bloke. Never had any problem with him. Only because I followed the rules."

"So, what do you think happened?"

"Well he sure as shit didn't drown," Reilly growled.

"What makes you say that?" Nash asked.

"Because I saw him the day he disappeared."

Nash leaned forward in his seat. "Tell me."

"He called in and checked my pumps on the way through to

Dawn Station. He'd called me the night before to let me know he was coming."

"Was that usual?" Nash asked.

Reilly shrugged. "Sure. I had nothing to hide. He knew that."

"Was he OK the day you saw him?"

The station owner nodded. "He was fine but was heading to Dawn Station because someone had complained about their pumping."

"What about it?"

"I'm not sure. It's funny though how they have five storages, twice the size of one of mine, and they're always full, but they still keep pumping."

Nash frowned. "Aren't there licenses or something like that for water rights?"

"They only work for those that respect them."

"Would they use that much water?"

Reilly shook his head. "They make more by selling it."

"How much more?"

The station owner blew out a long breath. He said, "A conservative estimate ... and I do mean conservative, would be three-hundred million dollars."

The PI almost choked on his beer. He coughed and said, "More than enough motive to kill someone for."

"As I said, he sure didn't die like they said he did."

"How do you know? No one has found him. He's still listed as missing."

"Because when I last saw him, he was headed back to town

in an awful hurry. And where they found his boat was in the opposite direction."

Things were just getting more interesting. "Did you tell the local law this?"

Reilly snorted. "I'd tell him shit. Everyone knows he's in their pocket."

"Whose pocket?" Nash asked.

"Dawn Station."

"Could he have come back later?" Nash asked.

"Ray?"

"Yes."

"No. It was almost dark when I saw him. It's not the best idea to travel the river at night."

"Did you see him clearly. You're sure it was him?" Nash pressed.

"Of course, I'm fucking…" Reilly stopped abruptly, glanced around and then lowered his voice. "Of course, I'm sure. There was something, now you mention it. He was hunched over. Not upright like someone would normally be when driving a dinghy."

Nash thought for a moment and then said, "If what you say is true, it's more likely that he was killed, and someone took the dinghy back downstream to where it was found."

"I told you he didn't drown."

"There is one other possibility," Nash pointed out.

"What?"

"He may have fallen out upstream and the boat drifted downstream on the current."

"I don't believe that. Do you?"

Nash shook his head. "From what I've experienced since I've been here, no. What can you tell me about Ringa and his mates?"

Reilly's stare grew hard. "You'd do well to stay away from them. They're trouble with a capital T."

"Too late on that front I'm afraid," Nash said and told him what had happened the previous night. "I'm trying to figure out where they fit into the picture. They're not farmhands by any stretch."

"Security," the station owner said. "Security and muscle. They run patrols around that property all the time. As well as the security cameras. Ray had been chased off that property more than once by them, trying to investigate rumours. Obviously, this time he found something, and they shut him up."

"I guess the question is, what did he find?"

"Your guess is as good as mine."

"One last question, Mike. If all their storages are full, where would all the water go that they're still pumping?"

"The aquifer."

Nash was surprised again. "What aquifer?"

"Under Dawn Station is a large aquifer. It's big enough to hold the equivalent of three more of their surface storages."

"That's a lot of water."

"Damn right it is."

"Is that what Ray was checking on the last time he was here?"

Reilly nodded. "Yes."

"Did you tell him about it?"

The expression on his face changed. "Yes. And it got him killed."

"Not your fault, Mike. Listen, wouldn't it show on their meters if they were pumping all that extra water?"

"It should, but it never did. Even after the pumps were running day after day."

"Did they disable the meters?"

"If they did, the meters were working fine when they were inspected."

"Which means they had someone tipping them off whenever an inspector was due."

"That would be my guess," Reilly agreed.

The door from the bar opened and two men walked through. Ringa and Jacko. Nash saw the look on Reilly's face and said, "Relax. I'll take care of it."

The pair of troublemakers walked across to their table. The new arrivals stared down at them, and Ringa said to Reilly, "You might want to be choosey about who you eat with, Mike. The smell of pig shit might upset your stomach."

Reilly's eyes narrowed. "You got some on your boots?"

Both Ringa and Jacko chuckled. Then he sneered, "What's the old fool been telling you, Nash? How all us on Dawn Station are bad dudes? About how we take all the water out of the river?"

"About how you killed Ray Petersen," Reilly growled.

Ringa glared at him and took a step forward. "You watch your mouth, old man. You might end up at the bottom of the river like the water guy."

Reilly made to get to his feet in a fit of rage, but Nash snapped, "Mike! Leave it!"

"Yeah, Mike, leave it," Jacko jeered.

Nash stared at them and said in a low voice, "It's time you blokes left."

"How about you just sit there and shut the fuck up," Ringa hissed. "This is between me and him."

"Well, I'm cutting myself in."

"Yeah?"

Reaching around behind him, Nash took the Glock from his waistband and laid it on the table. "You're leaving."

Ringa stared at the weapon and then said, "This ain't over pig."

"I don't expect it is."

The two men turned and left. Nash caught sight of Kerry watching from behind the lounge bar. The PI tucked the Glock back into his pants.

"Jesus Christ," Reilly hissed. "That was fucking heavy."

"Had to send him the message," Nash explained. "I suggest you go home, Mike. Stay there for a few days. I'd say things are about to get a little out of hand right quick."

"Do you need some help?"

"Nope. I've some experience with this kind of thing. Have you ever heard of a town called Katanka?"

Realization settled upon the station owner. "Are you him? The bloke who took on them bikies?"

"Yes."

"Well blow me down."

CHAPTER TWENTY

"Christ, Nash. Not only did you poke the bear, but you slapped it on the arse," Gloria growled. "And then you dropped out your dick and said, fucking match that."

To say Gloria wasn't happy about it was an understatement. Nash was expecting her to come through the phone at any point. He said, "Keep it down, Gloria, you'll wake the baby."

"I'll give you wake the fucking baby," she hissed. "You're up there on your own with no backup and you pull shit like this."

"It's fine," Nash tried to reassure her. "Besides, don't you want to hear what I have?"

There was a brief silence while Gloria calmed herself before saying, "Tell me."

"I found out that Dawn Station pump way more water than anyone else. Apparently, they have an underground aquifer on their land. All the water they have is worth hundreds of millions."

He went on to tell her the rest, including the part about Reilly seeing Ray Petersen later in the day.

"Someone went to a lot of trouble to stage the boat accident," Gloria surmised.

"The body has to be somewhere," Nash told her. "But locating it would be like trying to find a needle in a haystack."

"So, what are you going to do next?" Gloria asked him.

"On Monday I'm going to Dawn Station to have a look around."

"Is that wise?"

"Probably not," Nash admitted. "But I still need to see what's going on out there."

From outside came the sound of a gunshot, quickly followed by another. Nash got to his feet and hurried across to the window. He looked out and saw a cream ute, or it might have been white, start to speed away along the street with a squeal of tires. Then he saw the body lying beside a white Landcruiser. Reilly's Landcruiser.

"Shit!" he cursed.

"What is it?" Gloria asked urgently.

"I've got to go. I'll call you back."

Nash disconnected and rushed from his room. He ran along the hallway until he reached the stairs and took them in three bounds. Hitting the bottom at a dead run, he crashed out through the door at the front of the pub.

People were already starting to gather outside. He pushed

through the crowd and knelt beside the fallen station owner. "Mike, can you hear me?"

Reilly murmured something.

"Come on, Mike, stay with me."

Nash looked up at the crowd. "Did someone call an ambulance?"

They all looked at each other stupidly. "I did," a voice said.

"Hang in there, Mike," Nash urged him.

"Nash?" his voice was weak, garbled. "Is that you?"

"Yeah, Mike."

"The bastards got me."

"Who, Mike? Who was it?"

"It … I saw him. It …" Reilly slipped into unconsciousness.

It took the ambulance ten minutes to get there. By that time, Mike Reilly was dead.

Nash watched the paramedics load the body into the back of the ambulance and close the doors. As they pulled away, Royall appeared. His marked car pulled in to an empty parking space and he climbed from the driver's seat.

"Where the hell have you been?" Nash snarled.

"I was out of town when I got the call. How is he?"

"He's dead, that's how he is."

"Too bad," was all Royall said.

"Whoever it was that shot him, they were driving a white or cream-colored ute. It was hard to tell in the light."

"Did you get a number plate?"

"No. But surely you must have an idea? You do live here."

Royall shrugged. "There are a few around. But then again,

it could have been anyone passing through, too."

"I saw it," a man said and stepped forward. "It was a yellow ute."

"There you go," Royall said to Nash. "Three different colors from two different witnesses. My job just got really easy."

Nash stared at the man. He recognized him from the previous night. He was one of the crew who'd been with Ringa. "Did you happen to see the plate?"

The man shook his shaggy head. "Nuh. The taillights were too bright."

"Happy now?" Royall asked. "All right, everybody go home. Nothing to see here."

"Is that it?" Nash asked, bewildered and angry. "You're not going to set up a crime scene?"

Royall scowled at him. "Listen, Nash, out here we don't have all of the things you have in the city. So, we do things differently. Old school, by asking questions and legwork. Now get the fuck out of my face."

Officially Nash wasn't a cop, so there was little he could do. Instead, he turned away and stormed upstairs, slamming the door to his room so hard that one of the old pictures that held tenuously to a wallpapered wall, fell off its hook and smashed on the floor.

He reached into his pocket and took out his mobile. He dialed and Gloria's voice came across from the other end. "Nash, what happened?"

"Someone just shot the man I talked to earlier this evening. He's dead."

"Shit," she hissed. "This is getting out of control. Have you any idea who it was?"

"Yeah. Proving it though is a whole other issue," he told her. "Especially with Royall running the show."

"What's he doing?"

"That's just it, he's doing nothing."

"I'll make a call to see if there's anything that can be done."

Nash snorted. "By then it'll be too late."

"I'm sorry, Dave. But we've got to think of the big picture. Somehow, it's all linked together, and we've got to find it."

"It's not that hard, Gloria. It's water and money. They lose the water, they lose the money. Have you had any luck finding out who owns Dawn Station, yet?"

"No. It looks like Whitfield at the moment. Everything here seems to point to him."

"Then ask yourself this. Where would he get the money? Plus, he's the water minister. Wouldn't it be a conflict of interest?"

Gloria sighed. "Not if it can't be traced. Listen, I'll call you on Monday after I've been to Goulburn. Hopefully, it'll fill in a few blanks. You just find what you need and get out. And stay safe."

CHAPTER TWENTY-ONE

The mobile in Whitfield's pocket buzzed and he took it out. He saw the number on the screen and felt a wave of heat wash over him. If they were ringing him at this time of night, then it wasn't good.

He looked about the ballroom and saw his wife dancing with the boss of the Construction, Forestry, Mining & Energy Union (C.F.M.E.U.). She laughed at something the union boss had said and then they went back to talking while their feet took them around the floor.

He put it up to his ear. "Yes?"

"You need to reign your guys in," Royall said.

"Are you crazy?" he hissed. "Do you know where I am? I'm at a fucking C.F.M.E.U fundraising ball. Couldn't this wait?"

"One of your boys at Dawn Station just killed the owner of Piccadilly Station."

"Christ."

"Listen," Royall went on. "I can only do so much. But if your boys out here keep killing everyone they come across, we'll have more Feds crawling up our arses."

"What has Nash found out?"

"At the moment, not much as far as I know. But he was talking to the bloke right before your boys did their thing. You need to get your fucking house in order before the ceiling caves in on you."

"What can you do about the dead person?"

"For the moment it is a state law enforcement matter. So, I can go through the motions and leave it as an unsolved case. But the missing water inspector, that's federal. If Nash finds something on that, there's not much that can be done."

"Yes, there is."

"What?"

"Make him disappear too."

"I don't think you want to do that," Royall cautioned him. "That'll just cause more trouble. You think the director will like that?"

Whitfield's blood boiled. Through gritted teeth, he said, "I'll sort it out."

He hung up and hit speed dial one. The call connected. "Boss?"

"Mario, I want the helicopter ready to go first thing Monday morning," Whitfield said.

"Where we going?"

"On a little trip."

"Is there a problem?"

"Nothing that can't be sorted," Whitfield allowed. "Arianna will be coming with us."

"I'll take care of it."

Whitfield hung up and took a sip of his scotch.

"Is everything all right?"

He looked up from the table, into the smiling face of his wife Arianna. He smiled at her. "It's fine."

Peter Temple slapped him on the shoulder. "Hey, why the long face. Smile. This time next week, you'll be leading the country."

"We'll see."

"I have inside information that the numbers are swinging your way," Temple said. "Am I right?"

"Must you two talk politics when we're here to have fun?" Arianna asked.

Whitfield stared at her. The form-hugging black dress she wore was divine. It accentuated her curves and was cut low enough that the tanned tops of her large breasts were well exposed. Her long dark hair was down and framed her face perfectly. Then there were her eyes and lips. Rising from his seat, he said, "I'll be back in a minute."

CANBERRA
11:17 PM

Whitfield squeezed her throat with his left hand, his right crushing her right breast. She cried out as a trembling orgasm washed over her while he pumped vigorously from behind. She stiffened and then slumped forward towards the basin as he ejaculated inside of her.

The door to the toilets opened and a voice said, "Get your dick out of my secretary and get out here. The people have been waiting to hear you speak all night."

"Christ," Whitfield growled at Temple. "How about you knock next time."

Temple glanced at the tall blonde who was fixing her dress. "Mel, get out. The minister has work to do."

She gave him a wry smile. "After the way, he just screwed me, I doubt he'll have much energy left for work."

Mel walked towards the door and reached for the handle. She stopped and turned. "Give me a call, Mr. Prime Minister."

Whitfield stared at her and said, "Next week."

She opened the door and disappeared. Temple looked at Whitfield who was fixing his pants and snapped, "Are you fucking crazy. You get caught screwing around now and this whole thing blows up in your face. Say goodbye to The Lodge."

"It's fine, Pete," Whitfield growled. "And don't fucking talk to me like that."

"Someone needs to. What's wrong with your wife? If you want to get caught doing someone in the bathroom, why not her? Shit, I'd do her in here."

Whitfield stepped in so close that his nose was almost touching Temple's. His voice was icy when he said, "You don't mention my wife to me ever again. Understand?"

"Well ..."

Whitfield's eyes sparked and his nostrils flared. "Understand?"

"All right. Now, how about we go out and you talk to the crowd?"

CHAPTER TWENTY-TWO

Nash was out of bed early and dressed. He'd lain awake for a good portion of the night, mulling over everything that he'd learned so far. What irked him the most was the fact that nothing would be done about Mike Reilly.

He sat on the edge of the bed, trying to focus his memory on the ute he'd seen the night before. Yellow? In the glow the streetlights cast, he supposed it could have been, but he wasn't so sure.

"Stuff it," he growled and came off the bed. Stuffing the Glock down the back of his pants, he covered it with his shirt. Then he went downstairs and out to where Mike Reilly had been shot.

There was blood on the bitumen where the station owner had met his demise. Taking out his phone, he snapped a picture of it, then moved out onto the road and looked around. There were black tire marks on the road where the ute had spun them in their hurry to get away.

Nash took more photos. There wasn't much else to look at. Burnout marks and old pooled blood. Then something in the gutter caught his eye. He walked across and it became clearer. A spent brass casing. It looked to be 5.56 caliber.

He took a photo of it and then patted his pockets for something he could use to pick it up. Nothing. Looking about, he saw something in the gutter that he could use. A straw. Picking it up, he inserted the end into the casing. Lifting it up on the straw, he examined it. He'd been right. A 5.56mm round.

With it still on the end of the straw, Nash walked back into the pub. Instead of going upstairs, he entered the main bar area.

Cleaning up from the night before, Kerry was behind the bar. She saw him enter and stopped mopping the floor. "What do you want?"

He ignored her animosity and said, "I need your help for a moment if that is OK?"

"With what? I'm busy."

"Just a few simple things and I'll leave you alone."

"What do you need?"

"Let's see; cornflour, a lighter, ceramic bowl, knife, small brush of some kind, a candle, sticky tape, and a piece of white paper. Oh, plus another small bowl."

"Is that all? You don't want chips with that?" she asked with heavy sarcasm.

"How about bacon and eggs?"

"Caroline?" Kerry called out.

The younger sister poked her head around the corner. "Yeah?"

"Our friend here wants some breakfast."

"Sure."

She disappeared into the kitchen and Kerry followed her. Ten minutes later she reappeared with everything that Nash had asked for. "Why all this stuff, anyway?"

"I'll show you," he said in a mysterious voice.

Laying the shell casing on the bar, he picked up the candle and the lighter. Lighting the candle, he then took the ceramic bowl and waved the flame under underneath until the base of it was black.

"What are you doing?" Kerry asked again.

"Watch."

Once Nash was finished with the candle, he blew it out and used the knife to scrape the soot into the small bowl. He then repeated the step several times until he thought there was enough in the bowl.

Next came the cornflour. Placing some in the bowl, he mixed it together with the soot, then applied the mixture to the bullet casing, careful not to brush too hard with the small paintbrush.

"There," he said.

"What is it?" she asked.

"That is a partial fingerprint."

Kerry watched him closely as he took the sticky tape and

broke a piece off, placing it gently over the print. Lifting it away carefully, the homemade fingerprint powder came with it.

Lastly, Nash placed it onto the sheet of white paper. "There we go, all done."

"How'd you do that?"

"Watched a lot of McGyver when I was young."

Kerry gave him a questioning look.

"Never mind," he said, then touched his eye. "Your so-called boyfriend do that?"

She mumbled something and Nash said, "Brave man. Anyway, thanks for your help. Oh, do you have a small plastic sandwich bag at all?"

Kerry left the bar area once again and headed into the kitchen to get one. When she returned, she passed it to him and he took care as he placed the shell casing into it, then sealed it.

He took his piece of paper with the fingerprint and was about to walk off when he paused. Nash said, "Who was that bloke last night? The one who said he saw the ute?"

"Why?"

"You know who I am, don't you?"

She nodded. "He told me."

"Ringa?"

"He told me not to talk to you."

"Is that how you got the eye?"

A nod.

"Does he own a ute, Kerry?"

Nothing.

"What color is it?"

Still nothing.

"Who was the witness?"

Silence.

Nash sighed. "Who was he, Kerry?"

"Robbie Burns."

Kerry whirled and glared at her sister. "Caroline, no! Shut the hell up. If he finds out, he'll hurt you too."

"I'm not scared of him," she said with what Nash assumed to be false bravado.

"Where can I find him? Out at Dawn Station?"

Caroline shook her head. "He works in town at the garage. Porter's Paint and Smash."

"Damn it, Caroline," Kerry pleaded.

"That's all I want to know. Thank you."

Caroline disappeared and Kerry said, "You can't let him find out where you got the name from. He'll hurt her."

Nash nodded and said in a reassuring tone, "He won't find out from me."

"He better not, because if she gets hurt, I'll hurt you."

Nash turned away again and began to walk out. Caroline appeared with a plate of bacon and eggs. "Hey, you want this?"

"Give it to your sister. She looks like she could use the iron."

CHAPTER TWENTY-THREE

COLLARI
8:35 AM

Nash punched the number into his mobile and the call was picked up over eight hundred kilometers away in Sydney.

"No," the angry voice snarled.

"Come on, Smitty, I need your help," Nash said.

Wayne 'Smitty' Smith worked for the FSG, or the Forensic Services Group, and had on more than one occasion helped out Nash with some of his PI work. This time, however, he was having none of it.

"Fuck off, I'm not doing it," Smitty replied.

"It's a murder. I'm working with the Feds this time."

"I don't give two fucks, Nash. The last time I helped you, you dumped me so far in the shit that I almost drowned in the stuff. Get them to do it."

"I'll make it worth your while."

There was silence at the end of the line. At least he hadn't hung up.

"How about a 2009 Select NRL Classic Captain Signature Redemption Card? Robbie Farah?"

There was a growl in his ear. Smitty's weakness was his fondness for amassing Rugby League Collector cards. And Nash knew he didn't have the Farah one.

"Come on, Smitty. You're the only one I can trust. The Feds are leaking like a fucking sieve."

"Robbie Farah?"

"I swear."

"Shit. What do you have?"

"Hang on a moment."

Nash fumbled with his phone and then came back on the line. "I just sent you some pictures. The main ones I'm concerned about are the tire marks and the fingerprint."

More silence, this time from Smitty.

Then, "OK, I got them. Give me a couple of days and I'll see what I can do."

"You're a marvel, Smitty. I'll give you a number where you can reach me," Nash said and rattled it off.

"And you better come through or we're done," Smitty snapped and hung up.

COLLARI
9:03 AM

Nash parked the Landcruiser out front of the garage with blue and white paint peeling from its external walls. The sign above the double roll-a-doors read **Porter's Paint and Smash**.

He climbed out and made sure his Glock was within easy access then walked over to the glass shopfront door and tried it.

Locked.

He saw the red-letter sign stuck to the glass. **Closed**.

Bashing on the door, the glass rattling in the frame, he paused and then tried again.

No one was there.

"It won't be open until tomorrow," a voice said.

Nash turned to face an old lady who was dressed in her Sunday best. Maybe going to church, he thought.

"Would you know where I could find Robbie Burns?"

"Who, love?"

"Robbie Burns, he works here."

Shaking her head, she said, "Sorry, I've never heard of him."

She was about to keep walking when a thought popped into Nash's head. "Have you lived in Collari long?"

She frowned. "About thirty years. Why?"

"So, you'd be pretty familiar with most people around town?"

"Yes."

"Are there many people that drive white or yellow utes?"

"Four-wheel drives or ute, utes?"

"Ute, utes," Nash confirmed.

She looked thoughtful for a moment and shook her head. "No. There's no one that I recall who drives a yellow ute."

"OK."

"White ones, there's four that I remember."

"Really?"

"Yes. Fred Jenkins, Charlie Brown, don't ask me his real name, that's all I've ever heard him called. Who else? Um, Brian Davies, and that young man from Dawn Station."

Bingo!

CHAPTER TWENTY-FOUR

OUTSIDE COLLARI
9:36 AM

The Landcruiser hit another deep pothole with a loud crunch and caused Nash to grit his teeth in frustration. "Christ! You'd think someone would fix the damned road."

He'd left the bitumen about three kilometers back at the crossroads where the mailboxes and signs for Dawn Station and others were erected. The paddocks were dry, and it was obvious that it had been some time since they'd seen any rain.

The land was flat, sparsely littered with trees. Every now and then he saw a small herd of Droughtmaster cattle huddled under a gum, trying to escape the building heat.

Nash wasn't sure what he'd find out this way, but he wasn't about to sit around and do nothing. Feeling kind of responsible for Reilly's death, he had no intention of letting it go so easily.

Figuring that Ringa was the murderer, he kept asking himself why? Was it because Reilly had been talking to him. Or was it because the man from Dawn Station had been forced to back down? Or was it a message for him to back off?

And if it was ordered, then who ordered it?

Suddenly Nash slammed on the brakes, and the Landcruiser slid to a stop some twenty meters on. A red dust cloud enveloped the vehicle in an opaque mass. Before it had cleared, Nash had the Landcruiser in reverse.

The wheels spun and then bit as it lurched backward. He stopped at the thin sidetrack that branched away from the road and turned the wheel to the right and sent it forward onto the ribbon of dirt.

He followed it into a narrow stand of gums with a clearing at its center. Braking, he stared at the burned-out wreckage before him. Nash had found the ute.

Sliding out from behind the wheel, he walked over to the ute. Its blackened shell indicated that its maker was a Holden Crewman. The ground around it was scorched.

Nash walked around the front of it and tried the bonnet. It lifted away and underneath was just as bad as the exterior. He checked the firewall for the compliance plate, but it was missing, so he let the bonnet drop and cursed under his breath.

The sound of an approaching vehicle drew his attention back to the road. In the distance, Nash saw the rooster tail of dust thrown up by a speeding car. When it drew closer, Nash saw that it was a police four-wheel drive. It blew past the turn off which Nash had used and appeared to keep going.

That was until it slammed to a stop in much the same way as he had done. Then it started to back up.

"Shit," Nash cursed.

When Royall climbed out of the Triton, there was an angry expression on his face. He marched across to Nash and growled, "What the fuck are you doing out here?"

Your job. "I'm just out driving. Sunday is my day off. I happened to spot this burned out ute. Do you think it could be the one that was used last night?"

"It's been here a while."

Liar.

Nash shrugged. "OK then, I guess I'll be on my way."

Royall frowned at him. Maybe the sergeant had been expecting more of a fight. He said, "When are you leaving town?"

"When I've finished what I came here to do."

He was aware of Royall's burning hot gaze on his back as he walked to the Landcruiser. Climbing in, he started the motor but sat there for a moment looking at the police sergeant through the bug-smeared windscreen. It was like a stare off to see who would blink first, but after a short while, Nash got sick of it and drove off.

COLLARI PUB
10:57 AM

The Glock slid free of Nash's waistband and he brought it up. The door to his room was ajar and he distinctly remembered closing it and turning the key. With his left hand he gave the door a shove. It swung open with a low squeak until he could see all the way in.

Nash stepped across the threshold and swept the room. It was empty. And a mess. Someone had turned it over. Then it struck him why.

"Damn it!"

He walked over to the wardrobe where the spare pillows and blankets were kept. Its door was open, and the pillows were on the floor. The blankets, however, looked undisturbed, and he reached up and slipped his hand between them …

… and found nothing!

The bag with the bullet casing in it was gone.

COLLARI PUB
11:04 AM

There were only a few customers in the bar when Nash stormed in. Caroline was seated at a table, reading something, and there was a solidly-built man with dark hair behind the bar, pouring a beer. Nash walked across to Caroline and growled, "Where's your sister?"

She looked up at him and saw the anger in his eyes. "Kerry?"

"She's the only one you've got, isn't she?" Nash snapped.

"She's out the back."

"Where?"

"Hey," the man behind the bar placed the beer on the bar

and continued, "What do you want with my daughter?"

He ignored him. "Where?"

"Out at the line."

Nash pointed to the door above which was an exit sign. "Through that door?"

"Yes."

He headed towards the door and the man moved from behind the counter to cut him off. "I asked you what you wanted with my daughter?"

Nash was in no mood for messing around. "Get out of the way. You're obstructing a federal investigation."

"A what?"

"Move," his voice was low and full of menace.

The man stepped aside but followed Nash as he went outside. Bursting through the back door, he saw Kerry hanging out bar runners and handtowels. She saw him coming and a pained expression crossed her face. Nash's obvious anger made her automatically take a step back. As he closed on her, the first words to escape her lips were, "I'm sorry."

Grabbing her arm, he dragged Kerry toward him. "What are you sorry for?" he hissed.

"Hey, get your hands off my daughter," the man growled from behind him.

Without looking back, Nash pulled the Glock and pointed it at Kerry's father. "Back the fuck off or I'll have you arrested for interfering in a police investigation."

He couldn't but the threat had the desired effect.

"Kerry, who did you tell?"

"I ... I don't know what you mean?"

"Who did you tell about what I did this morning? Was it Ringa?"

"What are you talking about?" Kerry's father asked.

"This morning I found a shell casing in the gutter which I could link to the killer of Mike Reilly. I pulled a fingerprint from it. When I went out, I hid it in my room. When I came back, my door was open, and the room was turned over."

"No," the man gasped.

Nash's stare hardened on Kerry. "And guess what? The damned bullet casing is gone. Who did you tell?"

Kerry's thin wall crumbled. "He said he was going to hurt her."

"Who?"

"I had to tell him. If he found out ..."

"Who?"

"... he'd hurt her."

"Who, Kerry?"

"Ringa."

"Christ, why would you do that?"

"I told you, he would hurt Caroline."

"But he didn't know until you told him. The only way he *would* have found out is if someone told him. Now the only bit of hard evidence I found has gone."

"I'm sorry!" she half yelled.

Nash put the Glock away. "Yeah, so am I."

CHAPTER TWENTY-FIVE

Gloria walked into her office with the feeling that today would be the day things turned around. There were so many irons in the fire that something would surely turn up.

As she walked past Hoyland's office, he called out to her. She stopped and went back. "You rang, sir?"

"I want a briefing from you about where we're at, Gloria," he said. "I have to front the press at ten and then tell the Prime Minister where we're at. He's taken a personal interest in this."

"No problem. I'll fill you in before I head out."

He frowned. "Where are you headed?"

"Goulburn Hi-Max."

"The new prison?"

"Yes, sir, that's it."

He paused and said, "OK. Make sure you do."

"Yes, sir."

Gloria kept going and found both Annie and Leroy waiting in her office. She froze when she caught sight of her desk. "What the hell happened here?"

"I tidied it while I was waiting for you," Annie told her. "I'm sorry ma'am, but it was a fucking mess."

Gloria sat down in her chair and shook her head in disbelief. "No need to apologize. Unless I can't find anything. Now, what do we have?"

Leroy stood up and walked over to the whiteboard in the corner. He scribbled a name on it.

Tom Whitfield.

As he spoke, he wrote more. "We know that Flaherty worked for Whitfield at the time of the bombing in Orange. And this guy confessed to it."

He wrote another name on the board. Agostino Di Pietro.

"These are the two men he confessed to killing. Cristiano Ajello and Giacomo Cino."

"Italians? Who were they when they were alive?" Gloria asked.

Annie said, "According to the file, they were Whitfield's business partners. But before you came in, I did a little extra digging. They were fruit growers in the Orange area."

"OK. Nothing new there. A lot of Italians are fruit growers."

"The thing is, I managed to trace them all the way back to Griffith," Annie told her and let it hang.

"Griffith?" asked Gloria with an inkling of where this was leading.

"Yes, ma'am."

"Tell me more."

Annie glanced at Leroy. "You want to do this part?"

"You're doing just fine."

Annie continued. "After finding the Griffith connection, I put in a call to Organised Crime. I asked a few questions and was told that our dead friends, along with our confessor, were suspected of having links to the Italian Mafia. Not only that but to Guido Montanari himself."

"Holy shit," Gloria breathed. "Why is this only coming to light now? Why wasn't it in the original investigation file?"

"Maybe they never made the connection," Leroy suggested.

"Surely something must have popped though," Gloria said. "I mean, when they dug into their past, you'd think they would have found something?"

"Maybe they did," Leroy said. "Maybe they didn't put it in. After all, there were rumors about corruption in Orange at the time."

"That I already know," Gloria said and went on to inform them of what Nash had been up to.

"Have you heard from him at all this morning?" Leroy asked.

"No."

"I still think it was a mistake to send no backup with him."

Gloria ignored the comment. "Who investigated the bombing?"

"A detective called Williams."

"Leroy, find out where he is and call him. I want to know

all there is about the investigation."

"Let me know as soon as you do. Annie and I are going to Goulburn Prison to see our man."

"I'll get right onto it."

"Chase down the forensics on the Goulburn bombing too. I want to know for sure if our man is dead." She stood up from her chair. "Now I've got to go and fill in the boss about what we know."

CANBERRA
9:04 AM

Hoyland was on the phone when Gloria entered. He motioned to a chair and she sat while he finished the call. Once he hung up, he sighed and said, "Don't ever climb the chain of command, Gloria."

"I'll try to remember, sir."

"Where are we at?"

Don't tell Hoyland. "My team has a few leads and all of them point to one man. Tom Whitfield."

She waited for the explosion.

Instead, there was a soft, "Tell me about it."

"Our bomber worked on the man's property at the time the car bomb exploded in twenty-fourteen. A man named Agostino Di Pietro was convicted of the bombing. He confessed, actually. I don't think he did it. That's why I'm going to Goulburn. I want to question him."

"How is that relevant to our current situation?" Hoyland asked.

"The man in jail and the two who were killed were linked to the Italian Mafia in Griffith."

"Are you sure?"

"I aim to find out."

Hoyland sighed. "So, how is it linked to the situation with the missing water inspector?"

"I'm not sure. The only link is a supposedly bent cop by the name of Royall who was in Orange at the same time."

"So, what you have is a dead man who worked for Whitfield in twenty-fourteen, and a cop who was in Orange at the same time?"

"That dead man blew up a car with a senator in it," Gloria pointed out.

"And the only link to Whitfield is that he worked for him?"

"Yes, sir."

"Apart from the solid evidence on the bomber then, you've got stuff all."

"As I said, I'm hoping to find out more today."

"Let it go, Gloria," Hoyland said. "You've got your bomber. Be happy with that."

"But we don't know why," she pointed out.

"Tell me how this other thing with Nash is going?"

"Slowly, sir."

"Fine. Give him a couple more days and then pull him in. If he hasn't found anything by then he's not likely to."

"Yes, sir."

"And like I said, tidy up the loose ends and put this case to bed. You've got your man."

"I won't know that until I get the test results back."

"Fine, then do it."

"Yes, sir."

CHAPTER TWENTY-SIX

CANBERRA
9:10 AM

Leroy lifted the receiver from its cradle and punched in the number he'd been given. The connection clicked and rang three times before a voice answered. "Williams." The voice was low, gravelly.

"Is this Detective Sergeant Ben Williams?" Leroy asked.

"Speaking."

"This is Constable Leroy Mertens over at AFP in Canberra. I need to ask you some questions about a case you worked a few years back."

"Sure, which one?"

"The bomb that went off in Orange."

There was a brief silence and then, "What do you want to know?"

"I managed to get a copy of the file because a name popped

up in a case we're working, and we traced it back to Orange."

"What name would that be?"

"Michael Flaherty."

"Give me a minute while I reboot my brain." After a few more seconds of silence, Williams said, "Yeah I remember the name. Nothing was followed up on because of the confession of the other guy."

"What do you mean nothing was followed up?"

"You know how it is. Flaherty was there so we took his name for questioning. But we got a tip that it was this other bloke, so we picked him up and he confessed."

"Who'd you get the tip from?"

"Whitfield, the owner of the property. He told the Chief Superintendent who was on scene at the time."

"Did you do background checks on everyone? Even the dead?"

"Yeah."

"What did you come up with?"

Williams paused and then said, "Officially, nothing."

"Unofficially?" asked Leroy.

"I found connections," Williams answered.

"Uh-huh, so did we," Leroy acknowledged. "What was yours?"

"The two men who were killed, and the bloke who confessed, had links to the Italian Mafia."

"You found that?"

"Yeah."

Leroy's voice hardened. "Then why the hell wasn't it in the

report?"

"Because we had our man and a confession, and I was told to leave it out."

"Christ. Who the fuck told you to leave it out?"

"The Chief Superintendent, Pete Hoyland."

"Shit."

"Exactly."

CANBERRA
9:20 AM

Leroy caught Gloria about to leave her office. She'd picked up her handbag and keys and was walking towards the door when Leroy filled the space and blocked her path.

"You are not going to fucking believe this," he said in an excited whisper.

"Try me."

"I just got off the phone to Williams. You know, the bloke who investigated the bombing in Orange?"

"Yes, tell me something."

"He remembers the name of our bomber but never questioned him because there was the tip about the guy they fingered for it. That tip came from Whitfield himself."

"How convenient."

"But that's not all," he said with a smile.

There was exasperation in Gloria's voice when she said,

"Well, shit. Are you going to tell me, or do I have to guess?"

"Williams found the link between them and the mafia. It wasn't put in the file because he was told to leave it out."

There was more, Gloria could tell, and by the expression on Leroy's face, it was good.

"Who told him to leave it out?" she asked.

"The Chief Superintendent at the time."

"Christ, Leroy, give me a fucking name."

"Pete Hoyland."

"Shit!"

"That's what I said."

"Get Annie for me. Now."

While Leroy went to find Annie, Gloria dialed Nash. The phone rang twice, and he picked up.

"Morning, how're things?"

"I think I've done a bad thing, Dave," she told him.

"Tell me what and we'll see if we can fix it."

She told him about what they knew and about Hoyland. "I think he's the leak."

"Oh well, at least we know."

"He wants me to shut the investigation down after we get the results to confirm that Flaherty was killed in Goulburn. But now that I know about this other stuff, I need to speak to this witness in prison."

"So, what's the problem?"

"I told Hoyland I was going."

"Didn't you tell him you weren't going?"

"Not exactly, but I guess he could think that way."

"Then just go."

"Oh, I intend to."

"Stay safe, Gloria."

CHAPTER TWENTY-SEVEN

Leroy arrived back with Annie in tow and they closed the door to Gloria's office. She stared at her boss and said, "Leroy said you wanted me here."

"Did he tell you why?"

"No."

Gloria filled her in on what they now knew.

"Holy shit."

"That's what we said," both Gloria and Leroy said in unison.

"What are we going to do?" Annie asked.

Gloria said, "We're going to Goulburn Hi-Max. Leroy still has to chase down the results we're waiting on regarding the body, and then I want you to call Mack McKenzie at New South Wales Police Internal Affairs. I want to know if Hoyland ever came across anyone's desk. And if so, how did he ever get this job with the AFP?"

"You really want to do this, ma'am?" Leroy asked.

"Yes. Listen, while you're here you need to know something else," Gloria told them. She took a deep breath and said, "There is a leak somewhere in this office. They knew who Nash was when he arrived in Collari."

"Christ," Leroy hissed. "You figure with what we know, that it might be Hoyland?"

Gloria nodded. "That's why you need to be careful. We all do. From now on you only tell him the bare minimum or refer him to me."

"Won't he get suspicious?" Annie asked.

"It's up to us to make sure he doesn't."

"It's like running an investigation within an investigation," Leroy said.

"Something like that. But now that we know what we're up against, we might be able to use it to our advantage when the time comes."

Unless he catches us out and we wind up out of a job before we're finished. Or worse, Gloria didn't add. Then she said to Leroy, "Go and make that call to Mack, and find out if there is anything from the lab. We're leaving."

CANBERRA
9:50 AM

Leroy sat at his desk, staring at the phone. If he did what Gloria had asked him to do, then there was no coming back. He'd have to see it through to the end. Then again there was always the chance that someone would call Hoyland and tell him what was going on.

Instead, the phone came to him and he lurched in his seat when it rang. Snatching it up, he said, "Mertens."

"This is Mack McKenzie from New South Wales Internal Affairs. I was trying to reach Gloria Browning. I guess they put me through to you instead."

"That's OK," Leroy told him. "I was ordered to ring you. I guess you saved me the trouble."

"What about?"

"You first."

"Fair enough. Gloria asked me to run a check on a name she had come up. Do you know anything about that?"

"She might have mentioned it," Leroy said. Picking up his pen from the desk, he dragged a note pad closer to him. He flipped over a fresh page and waited.

"You got a pen?"

"Sure have."

"His name is Darrell Ring. He's ex-SAS and was dishonourably discharged three years ago. He did four tours of Afghanistan. Nasty piece of work. Apparently, he was investigated for shooting an unarmed civilian over there. They couldn't prove it without a doubt but discharged him anyway. If he's anywhere near Nash, then Nash needs to be careful. Not that I care, Ring can kill his fucking arse as far as I'm concerned."

"I'll let Gloria know."

"You do that. Now, what did you want with me?"

Leroy hesitated, opened his mouth to speak and then closed it again. He looked around his office as though there might be someone hiding there, listening.

"Mertens, you there?"

"I'm here. Listen, what I'm about to ask you can go no further, understand? There's a lot riding on this."

"Just ask me, son, and don't fuck around. I don't have time for this."

"The boss said she called you on the weekend about the case we're working, especially about Chris Royall."

"She did."

"And she said that he was also suspected of being bent. Is that right?"

"Yes."

Here we go. "Did the name Peter Hoyland come through there at any time?"

"I don't ..." a pause. "You did say, Peter Hoyland, right?"

"Yes."

Mack's voice lowered. "Fuck me. Are you people investigating your own boss now?"

"Short story, yes. He ordered the lead detective on the Orange bombing to leave the mafia stuff out of the case file. He is now keen to see that this bombing here is wrapped up quickly once we ID the bomber. And lastly, we have a leak and it points to him. So, you see why we need to know if he cropped up in your neck of the woods in the past."

"I'll say it again, fuck me. Listen, this is big bananas here, son. You want to be sure before you follow the rabbit down this hole."

"Gloria is," Leroy told Mack.

"Shit. Give me an hour and I'll get back to you."

"Just be careful," Leroy warned him.

"Don't worry, son. This isn't my first rodeo."

Leroy depressed the disconnect button and then punched in another number. It had only rung once when Hoyland appeared at his desk. Hanging the phone up, he said, "Can I help you, sir?"

"Yes, where's Gloria?"

"Her and Annie went out to follow something up."

"Will she be back soon?"

"Not sure. Maybe after lunch."

Hoyland nodded.

"Anything I can help you with, sir?"

"No, it's fine. Carry on."

Leroy breathed a sigh of relief when Hoyland disappeared.

CHAPTER TWENTY-EIGHT

FEDERAL WAY
10:20 AM

After leaving the office and climbing into an unmarked Commodore, Gloria had escaped Canberra by traveling along Kings Avenue, then Parkes Way, and getting off there onto Northbourne Avenue. From there the street turned into Federal Way, along which they were now traveling.

Rain started to fall on the windscreen and Gloria was forced to flick the wipers on. Intermittent at first, and then faster as the rain got heavier.

She glanced across at Annie who was staring out the passenger window at the drab-grey day.

"Penny for your thoughts," Gloria said.

"I guess it's starting to sink in just how big this thing is," Annie said. "Do you realize the shit storm this will cause if we can link a prospective prime minister to the Italian Mafia?"

"Not just that, remember," Gloria said. "Our boss is in this up to his nuts. He has to be."

Gloria's mobile phone rang. She hit the answer button and passed it to Annie. "It's Leroy, put him on speaker."

Annie did so and said, "Hi Leroy, you're on speaker."

"Hey, Annie. Boss, I talked to Mack and he said he'll get back to me so I'm just waiting for his call. Also, the boss was looking for you."

"Fuck it," Gloria hissed. "What did you tell him?"

"I just said you were out checking on something with Annie. Said you'd be back after lunch some time."

"OK. What about the results on our suspect?"

"I'm just about to call and give them a push. I thought I might phone Orange as well and see if they still have anything on the bombing back in twenty-fourteen. You know, signature, materials, shit like that."

"OK. Do it. We'll see you when we get back."

CANBERRA
10:25 AM

The call through to forensics turned up good. The results had just come through and most of the components and trace elements of the bombing in Goulburn matched the one in Canberra. Which was good because the person who'd set the bomb that had killed Colin Worth and his driver, had also set the bomb in Romana Fielding's office. Now all he had to do was see if anything matched the one in twenty-fourteen and things really would heat up.

His next call was to check whether there were any results on the corpse found in Romana Fielding's ruins. A young lady answered the phone. "Hello, Lara speaking."

"Lara, this is Senior Constable Leroy Mertens at AFP. I'm calling about an autopsy which was done on a body sent down from Goulburn."

"The bombing? Is that the one?"

"Yes, that's it."

He heard her shuffling around and then she came back to him. "I've got them here actually. Would you like me to send them over?"

"Yes, please. Um, could you answer me a couple of questions first?"

"Sure."

"Did you get an ID on the victim?"

"Yes. It came back as a Michael Flaherty," she told him.

"And cause of death?"

"Not the bomb, that's for sure. He was shot in the head."

"What kind of weapon?"

"We were lucky on that one. Although he was burned, he'd escaped the worst of the fire when part of the roof came down on top of him. I was able to pull the bullet from his head. It's a nine-millimetre."

"Fantastic."

"Not for him," she said.

"What? No, not that. If you could get them over right away,

that would be good, thank you."

"Consider it done."

The call disconnected and Leroy made his last call; to Orange. The phone rang twice, and a desk sergeant picked up. "Sergeant Collingwood."

"Sergeant Collingwood, this is Senior Constable Leroy Mertens from the AFP in Canberra, I was wondering if you might be able to help me out?"

"I'll do what I can."

"We're investigating the bombing of Senator Colin Worth and our prime suspect in the case seems to be linked to a case in twenty-fourteen on your patch. I was wondering if you might be able to dig into your files, find the right one, and email it to me, please?"

"All of it?"

"Yes, if that's possible?"

"I guess. But it will take a while to scan it all."

"Is there no electronic copy?"

"No, just the hard copy."

"OK, that would be great. But I still need something out of it like yesterday. Could you find me the report on the bomb itself and send it through straight away?"

"I'll do that and get the rest to you as soon as possible. Give me thirty minutes."

"Thanks."

The call disconnected and Leroy looked at his watch, already growing impatient.

CHAPTER TWENTY-NINE

Nash cut the engine on the dinghy and let it drift into the bank. Its nose dug into the earth and it shuddered to a stop beneath the outstretched limbs of a giant Rivergum. Somewhere above, a crow cawed; the guard dog of the bush.

Making sure he had his Glock, Nash climbed from the craft and tied it to a fallen log. Once it was secure, he waited for a moment, listening. All seemed quiet. The sound of birds in the trees and water lapping at the aluminium sides of the dinghy were the only things audible. He glanced at the six big water pumps a further sixty meters downriver to his left, and could fully understand how much water they could drain out of the river system.

Slowly, Nash climbed the riverbank until he was just below the crest. Between him and a massive cotton field was about five-hundred meters of full-grown Rivergums. He started forward, trying to keep trees between him and open space. When he reached the field, he stopped and looked about. To his left was an elevated farm track which ran down to the pumphouse. In the distance, approximately one kilometre from where he stood, was the homestead.

Nash turned left and headed towards the pump house. He needed to find the aquifer that Reilly had told him about, and the pumps were the most logical place to start.

Keeping to the trees, Nash made his way closer to them, moving cautiously, making sure he paused and listened for anything out of the ordinary. Eventually, he reached the pump site. The centrifugal pumps were housed under a large roof, not unlike a barn with no walls. When the water was sucked out of the river system, it was dumped into a deep channel that directed the water to one of the colossal dams on Dawn Station, which resembled large bays in the ocean.

However, there was one outlet pipe which didn't empty into the channel. This one cut across the paddock away from the rest. Immediately, Nash knew he had to follow it, and began walking, hugging the tree line.

The pipeline remained in sight for a while, but then cut away from the river at an angle and soon Nash realized that if he didn't leave the trees, he'd never find out where it led. *Shit.* After a moment's hesitation he stepped out into the paddock.

CANBERRA 10:55 AM

Leroy almost missed the call when it came through to his desk. He'd been taking a piss and by the time he returned, the phone had almost rung off the hook. Then he was stopped in his doorway by someone else looking for Gloria.

By the time his hand touched it, Leroy was sure he was too late.

"Mertens."

Collingwood said, "You are lucky, I was about to hang up."

"What have you got?"

"Those files you wanted should be in your inbox now."

Leroy said, "Thanks." And then hung up.

He sat down at his desk and opened his email, scrolling down until he found the one from Collingwood. He waited while the file opened and skipped to the last page to make sure they were all there, then pressed the print button. He ran to collect the sheets from the communal printer, then moved back to his desk and read through them, page by page. Picking up the newer bomb reports, he read through those as well, circling things as he went.

The similarities were there. By the time he'd finished, Leroy had five matches, right down to the type of explosive compound. He guessed Flaherty had a favourite substance. Which also meant that the guy in Goulburn Hi-Max was not the killer.

Leroy spent another thirty minutes going back over the reports to make sure everything lined up and that he'd missed nothing. It was still the same as the first time. Now he was more convinced than ever that Flaherty was in the frame for the Orange bombing.

For what felt like the hundredth time that morning, Leroy picked up the phone.

GOULBURN HI-MAX
11:25 AM

There was a special room at Goulburn Hi-Max where detectives and such could interview the inmates, away from the prying eyes of others. It was no bigger than an average-sized bedroom, with a table and four chairs. There were no windows, no two-way mirror, but there was a camera up in the right top corner which could record both visual and voice.

Gloria and Annie were waiting for a guard to show Agostino Di Pietro in when Gloria's mobile rang. She dug it out of her pocket and looked at the screen. "It's Leroy."

She pressed the answer button. "Make it quick, we're waiting on Pietro."

"When you see him, you might want to ask him why he lied to the police."

Gloria felt a chill go down her spine. "Hang on, I'll put you on speaker so Annie can hear."

She placed the mobile phone on the table and pressed the button. "Tell me more, Leroy."

"Pietro confessed to a crime he didn't commit. I had the

bomb evidence report emailed over and went through it alongside the one we have from Worth's car. Flaherty used the same explosive compound as he did in twenty-fourteen. Must've still had some just laying around."

"Shit. Good work, Leroy."

"That's not all, Gloria. Flaherty wasn't killed in the explosion. He'd been shot in the back of the head. A nine mil."

"Tying up a loose end," Gloria surmised.

"What do you want me to do with this info?"

"Just sit on it until we get back. We'll go from there. Have you heard from Mack yet?"

"No."

Gloria thought for a moment. "Leroy, do me a favour. Dig into Whitfield's background. See if there is anything that ties him to Griffith or the Italian Mafia."

"You think that there could be something there?"

"Well those blokes who were killed at his place in Orange had ties. What I want to know is if there's anything further back."

"Sure, no problem … Oh, shit!"

"What?"

"I forgot, when I spoke to Mack earlier, he found out about that Ring feller you wanted him to check on."

"Christ, Leroy."

"Sorry, boss, but I'm juggling a lot of balls at the moment."

"I know, what did he say?"

"His name is Darrell Ring, ex-SAS, dishonourably discharged after shooting an unarmed civilian in Afghanistan.

Not proven."

"Damn it, call Nash and tell him. Make sure he knows everything."

"Yes, ma'am."

"We'll talk when I get back. Bye."

Gloria hung up. She looked at Annie. "I have a feeling that this is going to be very interesting."

CHAPTER THIRTY

It was starting to get hot and the damned cicadas were letting Nash know about it. He figured that he was at least a kilometre and a half away from the river, and the pipeline was still traveling above ground. Off to his right was a high embankment, no doubt one of Dawn Station's water storages. A crow flew overhead and Nash wondered if the scavenger knew something he didn't.

The sat-phone rang and Nash stared at the number. Pressing the answer button, he said, "Hello."

"Nash? Leroy."

"What's up? Is Gloria all right?"

"Yes, she's fine. We got word on that bloke you were asking about. Ring?"

"Ringa."

"That's him," Leroy said and went on to tell him what Mack had told him.

"I guess that puts him in the frame for killing the old feller I was talking to. I reckon he's in it for the missing water inspector, too." Nash kept walking.

"Where are you?"

"In a fucking paddock on Dawn Station. I'm following a pipeline which I'm reasonably sure pumps water into an underground aquifer."

"Shit, man. Don't get caught."

"If I do, you'll know where to start looking."

"How's things your end?"

"Gloria is over at Goulburn. You knew she was going?"

Nash stumbled over a clod of dirt and then righted himself. "Fuck."

"What was that?"

"Yeah, I knew that. Something about a bombing in Orange."

"That's right. Only thing is, the feller she's going to question didn't do it. The bomb which killed Worth was the same compound as the one which blew up in Orange."

Nash stopped. "So that means that Flaherty did them both."

"Yep."

"Gloria wants me to dig into Whitfield's background and see if he can be tied to the Italian Mafia further back."

"What about Hoyland?"

"That's still a work in progress."

"Does he know what I'm doing today?"

"No, ever since we found out that he worked in Orange, we've been playing our cards close to our chest."

A plan started to form in Nash's head. He knew it was stupid. Probably shouldn't even put voice to it, but he did. "Leroy, give me half an hour and then tell Hoyland where I am."

Leroy almost came through the phone. "Are you crazy? That's suicide. Gloria will have my balls if I do that."

"Then don't tell her. I'll be fine."

"Shit, Nash, you really are fucked up."

"Do me a favour. Do you know Smitty? Works at FSG."

"I think so."

"Good. Give him a ring and ask him about some prints I'm waiting on, will you?"

Leroy shook his head. "I'll do it, but you're still fucking crazy."

MONTANARI FARMS
GRIFFITH 11:42 AM

The Bell 429 Global Ranger touched down smoothly, and the pilot eased the power down almost immediately. The doors opened and Whitfield, along with Arianna and Mario disembarked and walked across to the waiting black Range Rover. They climbed in and drove the two-hundred meters to the enormous Montanari homestead.

"I need to talk to your father before I come inside, Arianna," Whitfield said to his wife. "Business."

"It's always about business, Tom."

He bristled. "It's the fucking job, Arianna. You know that."

She pouted and bit her lip. He sighed. "I'm sorry. There's a lot going on at the moment. And if I get elected to replace the current prime minister, it's only going to get worse."

"Then don't do it."

"But it's what we've worked for."

"What my father has worked for, you mean?" she spat.

He let it slide as the vehicle swung around to a stop on the white gravel drive. The house had a huge veranda that swept around all sides, and four people were on the steps, waiting to meet them. One was Arianna's mother, Elena. The three men included her father, and his two hand-picked bodyguards, Enzo, and Ermanno. Heckle and Jekyll was more like it.

They climbed from the Range Rover and Arianna was the first to greet her parents. Hugging and kissing, they swapped small talk before her mother led her inside.

Guido came down the stairs and held out his hand for Whitfield. "Thomas, it is good to see you. What is this visit about?"

"Might we speak in private, Guido?"

Guido wasn't a tall man, but he was round. Not obese, but well on his way, due to his wife's cooking. A meal at the Montanari's would feed a homeless person for a week. A smile split his moon face as he said, "Of course, my son. Anything for the future prime minister of our fine country."

Whitfield never once let the smile fool him. Beneath the jovial exterior was a heartless killer who furthered his business by any means necessary.

They walked a short distance away and Guido said, "There. Now, what is it you wish to discuss?"

"There have been some issues."

Guido just stared at him and waited.

"The police who are investigating the bombing are getting close. They found out about the man I had do it."

"Did you fix that problem?"

"Yes, I had Mario kill him."

"Then there is no problem."

"Eventually they will work out that he worked for me. They are close, my contact on the inside has been keeping me informed."

"Uh, huh. Pay him more money, tell him to make it go away."

"Then there is the problem at Dawn Station."

Guido's face dropped. This could change everything. Dawn Station was where he was making his money. If that went away, then so did hundreds of millions of dollars. "I thought that was dealt with?" he hissed.

"That part was. The same people who are investigating the bombing have sent an undercover cop up there to nose around. I told the men up there to scare him off. All they did was shoot some old feller he'd been talking to."

"About what?"

"I don't know."

Guido's eyes blazed. "This is not fucking good, Thomas. If all these fuckups cost me my money, I'm going to look for someone to blame. And we know who that someone is."

"I can't just go and kill some federal cops, Guido."

"Why not? You had the senator killed."

"Killing cops is different."

"Then find another way. Do they have a family? Find them. Use them to send a warning."

"I'll look into it."

"Don't look, Thomas," Guido snapped. "Fix it."

"Yes, sir."

"And tie off any loose ends you need to. We are too close."

"Yes, sir."

"Look out there at my fruit trees. They are not doing so well this year. It may be time for some more special fertilizer to help them along."

Whitfield remained silent. He knew what Guido was on about. He'd seen the old bastard do it. One of his business associates had been taking one percent off the top of his profits, so Guido had shot the man himself and then had him fed into a woodchipper to fertilize the fruit trees.

Guido sighed. "Do not let me down, Thomas. Do not let me down."

CHAPTER THIRTY-ONE

Agostino Di Pietro had done his time so far, hard. His hair had all but gone grey. Weight had fallen off him, and deep lines were etched in his weary face. In other words, Pietro had aged considerably since he'd been locked away.

He stared at Gloria and asked, "Who are you?"

"Sergeant Gloria Browning, AFP. My friend here is Constable Annie Long."

He turned away and began shuffling towards the door. "Go away."

"We'd like to talk to you, Agostino. Just a few questions."

He kept walking towards the guard who'd brought him in. "I have nothing to say."

"Well I do," Gloria snapped. "Tom Whitfield."

Pietro stopped.

"Michael Flaherty."

He turned. Gloria could see the pain on his face. "Take a seat."

The man did as he was told, and Gloria looked at the guard. "We're right here."

"I can't leave, ma'am."

"Yes, you can, there's the door."

The guard shrugged and stepped out through the exit Gloria had indicated. Once he was gone, she concentrated on the man seated at the table. "We know you didn't set the bomb which killed Cristiano and Giacomo in Orange in twenty-fourteen."

His stare was unblinking. "That's not what the jury said."

"That's because you confessed," Annie pointed out.

"That's because I did it."

"Bullshit," Gloria snapped. "We know that it was Flaherty."

Pietro's face remained passive. "If you say so."

"What we want to know," said Annie, "is why? Why was it done and why did you confess?"

"Because I did it."

Annie sighed and climbed from her chair and walked around to stand beside him. She leaned down and said in a soft voice, "Bullshit."

Gloria studied his face. "Who are you scared of? Whitfield? Or Guido Montanari?"

His eyes flickered.

"So, it's Guido?"

"I didn't say that."

"We know it wasn't you, Agostino. We've told you that.

We have proof. Eventually, they're going to let you out of here. How's Guido going to take that?"

Pietro went silent again, but she could see the worry in his eyes. "We can protect you, you know."

"No, you can't. If I say anything, they'll kill my family."

"Who will? Guido?"

"Whitfield."

"No, he won't. I can promise you that. Your only hope is that you trust us. Like I said, either way, you're getting out of here soon. You can go it on your own and hope they don't come after you, or you can take up our offer."

Pietro's shoulders slumped. "OK. I'll tell you what you want to know."

He told them about the meeting and about how Whitfield had confronted him about skimming money. Then he told them about the bomb. He didn't know who'd planted it in the car, just that when Whitfield called, he'd had to confess that he'd done it. It was either that or they would kill him and his family.

"What was the meeting about?" Gloria asked.

"It was to discuss a new venture in which a lot of money could be made. He mentioned something about buying a cotton farm and how millions could be made from selling the water allocated."

"Where?"

"He didn't say."

Annie walked back around the front of the table and sat down. "Why did he kill the other two if it was just you who was skimming money?"

Pietro shrugged. "I think that came from Guido. We were his business partners. We were all skimming. With us out of the way, he had it all to himself."

Gloria took a moment before she asked another question. "Did the Orange police investigate it to the full?"

"The detective who was doing it didn't have to. Not with my confession. But there was something else he discovered while he was looking."

"The Mafia connection?"

"Yes. But his superior officer told him not to take it any further since they had their man. Me."

"Do you know who that was?"

Pietro stared at her thoughtfully and then nodded. "His name was Hoyland. Whitfield was paying him and another policeman off. I think his name was Roy or something like that."

"Royall?" asked Annie.

"Yes, that's it."

Gloria and Annie looked at one another. Gloria asked, "Agostino, we'll need you to say that in court when the time comes. Can you do that?"

Pietro paled at the thought of it, but he knew he didn't have a choice. "All right. But you have to protect us."

"It'll take a day or so to get everything sorted," Gloria told him. "But we should be able to fix it."

"OK. But don't leave it too long. They have people everywhere."

"Who, Whitfield?"

"No, the Italian Mafia."

CHAPTER THIRTY-TWO

Leroy still had doubts. He'd gone over what Nash had told him to do, time and time again. And he still came up with the same answer. Nash was fucking crazy, and Gloria would cut his balls off. Now he took the long walk to Hoyland's office to tell him about Nash.

At least the half-hour he'd waited had been productive. He'd called Smitty and found out that Nash had used some nifty shit to get him a fingerprint sample. The name it had been attached to was Darrell Ring.

Smitty had said, before hanging up, "You make sure Nash doesn't forget that he owes me."

Little did he know that after today, Nash would probably be dead, and he'd never see it. Goodbye career.

Leroy knocked on Hoyland's door and entered. His commander looked up from his paperwork and saw him standing there. "Mertens. What can I do for you?"

"I was wondering if you'd seen Sergeant Browning, sir?"

Hoyland frowned. "No. Not since this morning. Isn't she back yet?"

"I guess not."

"Is there anything I can help you with?"

"It's nothing, I guess. I just had a call from Nash. He's out at Dawn Station following something up. He was looking for the sergeant. I'm not sure if he had something or not."

Hoyland's face remained unreadable. He just nodded and said, "Well, when she gets back in, if I see her first, I'll let her know."

"Yes, sir."

Leroy turned and left the office, his guts churning. *What the fuck did I just do?*

When he got back to his desk, he dialled the satellite phone. "Hello?"

"It's me. I just talked to Hoyland."

"How did he react?"

"Didn't bat an eyelid."

"All right then. I guess we'll see soon enough, huh?"

"There's one other thing. Your friend Smitty came through."

Although he couldn't see, Leroy could tell Nash was smiling by the tone in his voice. "I knew he would. What did he say?"

"The fingerprint matched to one Darrell Ring. You watch your ass out there. You're carrying, right?"

"Yes. I'll be fine. Now let Gloria know."

"Sure. Just what I need, a great hunk of flesh chewed out of my ass."

"Put it this way, it'll draw Hoyland out and then she'll know for sure."

"Too bad you'll be all fucked up."

COLLARI
12:20 PM

"Sergeant Royall speaking."

"You've got trouble. Nash is out at Dawn Station."

"Why aren't you ringing them?"

"Because it would show on phone records, idiot. This way it will show I called your station. I can pass that off as a general inquiry."

"What do you want me to do about it?"

"Get the hell out there before they find him and kill him. Or do you want the whole of the AFP camped on your doorstep?"

"Maybe it might be better if he disappeared."

"Idiot. Find him and lock him up. Then call me and I'll have him recalled. The damned bombing case down here is all but closed anyway. Flaherty is dead. Caught up in his own damned explosion. So, just do what I say. Find Nash and bring him in."

"All right, damn it. I'll head out there now."

"Don't screw this up. And for Christ sakes, don't let that stupid fucking gun nut do anything."

"I'll see what I can do," Royall said and hung up.

Easier said than done.

FEDERAL WAY
12:32 PM

The white plastic guideposts flashed by with boring monot-
ony. The rain had gone and was replaced by bright sunshine.
Gone were the heavy grey clouds, with intermittent white
cotton balls in their place.

Before Gloria and Annie had left, they'd organized for Pietro to be put into protective isolation. All that had to be done
now was to convince the brass that he and his family were
worthy of protection.

The phone rang and Annie answered. She listened for a
moment and said, "You tell her."

She put it on speaker and Leroy said, "Nash called."

"How's he doing?"

"How did the interview go?"

"Good. I'll fill you in when we get back. How is Nash?"

"He's all right, for the moment."

"What is that supposed to mean, Leroy. What aren't you
telling me?"

"He had this crazy plan to draw Hoyland out."

"Oh, God. Do I want to know?"

"I told Hoyland that Nash was on Dawn Station."

Gloria slammed on the brakes and drove the car off the side

of the road. She ripped on the handbrake and shouted at the phone, "You did fucking what?"

"It was his idea. He said it would draw Hoyland out and then you would know for sure. He said he'd be OK."

"Christ, Leroy! Don't you know that Nash is fucking unstable?"

"I don't think he is, ma'am. It kind of made sense."

"Shit. Now I'm going to have to drive up there and hope like hell that it's not too late. This conversation is not done, Senior Constable," Gloria snapped and hung up.

"Nash can look after himself, can't he?" Annie inquired.

"It's not him I'm worried about. It's the trail of bodies he'll leave in his fucking wake."

She took the handbrake off, slammed the shift into drive, and scorched rubber as she took off towards Canberra.

CANBERRA
1:03 PM

Gloria threw everything she thought she'd need into a large bag, including an M4 carbine and extra magazines. It was hidden under her clothes and a few other things she'd thrown in. If command ever knew she kept it, they would hit the roof. But after several undercover stints, she'd made more enemies than she cared to have, and it made her feel safer just in case any of them came knocking on her door.

After dropping Annie off at headquarters with the instructions of telling Hoyland she was headed to Sydney to follow a lead, and for Leroy to organize protection for Pietro, she had driven home to pack her shit. She was still angry, but it was slowly ebbing and turning to concern. Old feelings for Nash began to resurface and it confused her. She thought they had long gone.

Before starting to pack, she'd called her babysitter, an ex-cop called Pearl Wilson, who was the only person she really trusted to take care of Rachel. She tried Nash's sat-phone again and got no answer. "Fuck you, Nash. Why do you do stupid shit?"

There was a knock at the door. She hurried to it and looked out the side window. Smiling, she swung the door open. Pearl stood there with Rachel in her arms. As soon as the little girl saw her mother, she gave her a huge grin and called out, "Mummy!" Gloria reached out and took her in her arms.

"I'm sorry to do this to you, Pearl."

They walked into the living room together. "It's fine, Gloria. It's the job."

"Are you sure you don't mind staying over? I just think she'll be more settled here."

"It's fine. You go catch bad guys. I'll take good care of our girl."

Gloria kissed Rachel on the cheek and said, "You be a good girl for Pearl, OK. Mummy will be back before you know it."

She handed Rachel back to Pearl and grabbed her bag off the floor. "Thanks, Pearl."

CANBERRA
1:10 PM

The phone handset flew across the room and hit the wall, smashing on impact. *"Fuck!"*

The shout must've echoed throughout the floor because almost immediately, Annie appeared in the doorway. "What's wrong?"

Leroy motioned for her to close the door. Once it was done, he said in a low voice, "Someone just killed Pietro. Stuck him about twenty fucking times. They couldn't save him."

"We were told that they were going to put him in solitary," Annie said in disbelief.

"They did."

"Shit, what now?"

"We go with what we have. Do you have a recording of the interview?"

"Yes, it's in my desk."

"Keep it safe. We may not be able to use it because he can't be cross-examined, but we might be able to use it in our statement."

"I'd better tell Gloria."

"Better you than me. I'll be on her shit list for life."

"You know he's the father of her child, don't you?"

"What?"

"She got pregnant when she was undercover with the Outback Animals. They both had no idea that the other was a UC.

Anyway, she got pregnant and had Rachel."

"Does Nash know?"

Annie shook her head. "Not as far as I know."

She reached for the phone and realized it was gone. "Where's your phone?"

Leroy pointed at the shattered handset on the floor. She raised her eyebrows. "I guess you're having a bad day."

Annie took out her mobile. She punched in Gloria's number and then proceeded to tell her the bad news.

CHAPTER THIRTY-THREE

DAWN STATION
1:26 PM

In the end, it wasn't a tip-off that did it for Nash. It was the hidden CCTV cameras around the station. But at least he'd found out where the pipe went before they found him.

He followed it for a further twenty minutes and then it just stopped, dropping at a right angle into the ground. It was well camouflaged. The pipe ran all the way to its destination behind a bank of earth. Anyone looking wouldn't see it.

Now that he knew the location of the aquifer, Nash contemplated sitting and waiting for them to come for him. Surely by now, they knew he was there. Then he thought better of it. If he was found near the pipeline, they might just shoot him on sight. So, he started across the paddock in the direction of the homestead.

Ten minutes later, two white Landcruisers came bouncing

across the paddock. One was a tray back, the other a five-door. They kicked up a large rooster tail of dust behind them that rose into the air like a bushfire really starting to burn. Nash reached behind him and felt for his Glock. He brought it out and stood there, slightly turned with it resting at his side.

No use letting them think he was a pushover.

The vehicles slid to a halt and the following dust plume swept over them. Men literally leaped from the cabs and spread out in a line to Nash's front. There were four of them. When the dust had cleared enough, he recognized two of them; Ringa and Jacko. Every single one of them was armed. Three had rifles. Nash figured they were .223s. Also, there were handguns tucked into their belts.

However, it was Ringa who commanded his attention. He was armed with an M4 carbine and it was pointed straight at him.

"You blokes look like you're kind of serious," Nash said.

"Serious enough to bury you out here," Ringa said.

"Are you the one in charge?" Nash asked.

"Yeah, I look after things," Ringa sneered.

Shaking his head, the PI said doubtfully, "No you're not. Someone with your temperament couldn't run this place. You're too cranky. Too hot-headed. Someone else calls the shots out here. How did you know I was here?"

Jacko smirked. "CCTV."

"So, what now, you shoot me for trespassing?"

Ringa nodded. "Something like that."

"Are you going to do it, or is it just women you're fond of doing over?"

Ringa took two steps forward and raised the butt of the M4. He was about to hit Nash a savage blow between the eyes when he was suddenly staring down the barrel of Nash's Glock.

The PI smiled. "Oops. Fucked that up, didn't you?"

With a muttered curse, Ringa lowered the carbine. But Nash didn't lower the Glock. He kept it right where it was, aimed at the centre of Ringa's face. "If you're going to waylay someone with the intention of killing them, then you really should check to see whether they're armed."

"Your life ain't worth shit, Nash," he cursed. "Jacko and the others will shoot you down like the dog you are."

"It won't matter much because you'll be dead."

Ringo's eyes narrowed. "Shoot him, Jacko."

There was a hesitant note in the man's voice. "Ringa ..."

"Do it!"

Nash tensed. He had no qualms about putting a slug in the bastard's head, especially if he kept going the way he was. He tried another approach. "I tell you what, Jacko. You ever hear of the Outback Animals?"

"Maybe."

"Stop talking and shoot the fucker, Jacko. Christ."

"I killed four guys that day," he paused to let it sink in. "Oh, look. There's four of you. They had the drop on me too. Only one difference, they'd already beat the shit out of me. Doesn't bode well for you guys, does it?"

The uncertainty was more visible now. Not just on Jacko's face, but on those of the other two as well. "Now, make up your mind. What's it going to be?"

The four of them never knew how close Nash came to pulling the trigger because the noise of another vehicle interrupted proceedings. Nash glanced and saw another Landcruiser bouncing over the paddock. This one was different, though. It had red and blue lights on its roof.

It skidded to a stop and two doors flew open. Royall appeared from the driver's side, his sidearm drawn and pointed at Nash. "Put the gun down, Nash!"

"What, so you can shoot me?"

Royall holstered his gun. "No. I'm going to take you back to town."

Nash glanced at the second man. Frowned. Then let his gaze linger longer. He knew this guy. It took a while to come to him but eventually, it did. Dario Laterza. One-time accountant for the Italian Mafia. He'd dropped off the radar just before Nash went undercover with the Devils. A little older maybe, but it was him.

"Let me have the gun, Nash," Royall said. "Can't have you shooting these boys."

"How about I keep the gun and I go to town with you anyway?"

Royall looked at the others. "All right. We'll do it that way."

"No!" Ringa snapped. "Royall, he ..."

"Shut up. You're lucky he didn't kill you," Royall snapped. He looked at Jacko. "Bring his boat back to Collari. I presume it's down on the river."

"It is," Nash confirmed.

"Well OK then, get in the four-wheel drive."

Nash tucked the Glock into his belt and did as he was told. As he walked past Laterza he said, "G'day Dario. How's it hanging?"

As they bounced across the paddock, Royall said, "You're nothing but damned trouble, Nash. Why the hell are you out here anyhow?"

"Just looking."

"Looking for what?"

"Ray Petersen."

"There? You think he's there?" Royall shook his head. "He drowned. His body is probably halfway to Bourke by now."

"He didn't drown, Royall. He was murdered. Just like Reilly was murdered. And it all ties into Dawn Station."

"You're crazy."

"How did you know I was out here?"

The question took him by surprise. "What?"

"How did you know I was out at Dawn Station?"

The answer took too long to evolve but Nash let it go. It gave him what he wanted to know. "Someone saw you leave the boat ramp. They figured where you were going and reported it to me," he lied.

"Lucky for me then, wasn't it?"

CHAPTER THIRTY-FOUR

COLLARI
2:30 PM

The hard muzzle of Royall's gun in his back made Nash freeze. He figured that being in town would make him safe enough. Maybe he was wrong. He felt the Glock leave his belt and then the sergeant said, "I'm locking you up. Then I'm going to make a call to your boss. Maybe he can reel you in."

"My boss is a woman."

Royall pushed the gun harder into Nash's back. "Move."

Once he was inside, Royall locked him in one of the two empty cells. "I'll have one of the girls from the pub bring you a meal."

"Don't overexert yourself," Nash growled. "Do I get a phone call?"

"We'll see."

The sergeant locked the door, and Nash looked around the

cell. It was small and smelled like someone had chucked up in there recently. The toilet was made of stainless steel and had no seat. Screwing up his nose, he thought, *Oh well, it could be worse. He could be taking a dirt nap.*

COLLARI
3:43 PM

The door to the cell opened and Royall appeared. He held up a phone and smiled grimly. "It's for you."

"Who is it?" Nash asked.

"Just take the damned thing."

He reached out and took it, hoping that it would be Gloria. It was Hoyland. "What in God's name are you doing, Nash? You were sent up there to look around quietly. Don't you know the meaning of the word undercover?"

Nash bristled. "This op has been fucked from the outset. Somewhere there's a leak. Not just a small one either. A gigantic fucking gushing one. They knew I was coming. And the only guy I talked to about everything was damn well murdered."

"Not my fault, Nash," Hoyland snapped. "Anyway, you're done up there. As of tomorrow, you're coming back to Canberra."

"I'm not done!"

"Yes, you are."

The phone disconnected and Nash stared at Royall who

smirked at him. Instead of saying anything, Nash started to dial a number.

"What do you think you're doing?"

"Are you letting me out?"

"Tomorrow."

"Then I get my phone call."

When he was finished, the call connected and the phone on the other end rang. "Hello?"

Nash stared at Royall.

"What?"

"Hello?" the voice said again.

Still Nash stared.

Royall muttered something and disappeared.

"Hello?"

"Yeah, it's me."

"Nash?" Gloria sounded relieved. "Shit. You're still alive."

"I'm in the Collari jail."

"Why?"

"It worked," he said in a low voice.

"What did? Hoyland ratted you out?"

"I think so. They're letting me out tomorrow and I'm headed back to Canberra. Your boss has terminated my assignment."

"Sit tight, Nash," Gloria explained. "I'll be there tonight. I'm on the road as we speak."

"I don't plan on going anywhere."

SYDNEY
4:03 PM

Mack was starting to get pissed off. His current mission had taken him away from other stuff and all he seemed to be doing was running into dead ends. That was until he found the file buried deep and out of sequence with others. He looked at the number at the top of it and typed it into his computer.

*Not Found!

He tried again.

*Not Found!

He ran a hand vigorously through his black hair in frustration. By rights, it should be there. If it was on paper, it should be in the computer. Which he took to mean that someone had buried the hardcopy file and forgotten about it and erased the electronic one.

Mack opened it and the first thing he saw was a picture of Guido Montanari. This immediately got his attention. The next picture in the file was that of Montanari's accountant, Dario Laterza. Mack knew of this guy because he'd been out of circulation for a while. They'd linked him to the payments of some corrupt police officers but then he'd just fallen off the face of the earth.

He kept sifting through until he found the paperwork pertaining to the bombing in Orange. Reading through it, two names stood out immediately. Royall and Hoyland. Then there was the third name. The one that made his mind race. Tom Whitfield.

"Fuck me," he hissed.

He looked for the creator of the file, who'd gathered the evidence that was in it. When he found the name, Ian Collier, Mack slumped back in his seat. Collier was dead. Car crash two years ago. His eyes danced over the photos and notes. This was the reason that there was no electronic file. Collier had been putting the evidence together himself. Which was why the file wasn't where it was supposed to be.

Then there was the one that stood out more than the others. The headline on the paper cutting read: *TOM WHIT-FIELD ELECTED BY A HUGE MARGIN!*

There was a circle on the page. Not around Whitfield, however, but around the wife. *Why would Collier circle the wife?*

Mack leaned forward and punched a few buttons on the keyboard. The file for Collier came up. He opened it and went through the pages. The Internal Affairs officer had died in an accident after his car ran off the road. According to the report, there was nothing conclusive to explain what had caused the accident. The only anomaly was a small patch of black paint on the corner of the rear bumper, which was passed off as possibly having been picked up in a carpark accident.

The coroner's report read: "*Accidental Death!*"

"Bullshit!" Mack snapped out loud.

He went through until he found the pictures of the car. It was a total wreck. It looked as though they'd had to cut Collier free. The car had hit a big tree just off the side of the road. He sat staring at it with brown eyes, searching as though it would tell him something. What was it saying? A picture tells a thousand words?

And it did.

It was right there in the background.

The sign in the paddock.

It said: ***ORANGE 5km***.

A coincidence? Highly doubtful.

He picked up the phone and called Leroy.

CHAPTER THIRTY-FIVE

CANBERRA
4:20 PM

"Here's the paperwork you wanted me to look at," Annie said, dumping it on Leroy's desk. "Fat lot of good it was."

Leroy looked up from what he was doing. "Have you heard from Gloria?"

"Not a thing."

"What about Hoyland?"

"I think he was finishing early. Something to do."

The phone rang and Leroy cursed softly. "This thing has been ringing its tits off all day."

Annie smirked. "Better its than mine."

It was an automatic reaction. Leroy looked up at Annie's breasts. "Gotcha," she chuckled.

"Crap," he muttered and picked up the new handset that Annie had found for him. "Leroy."

"Mertens? Mack."

"Mack? Damn, I'd almost forgotten about you."

"Yeah. I've been running down that thing for you most of the afternoon. Really screwed my schedule up."

"Sorry about that."

"Tell me you're not investigating Tom Whitfield in this shit."

Leroy remained silent.

"Christ, you are? You kept that quiet."

"No one knows."

"Well, then, what I'm about to tell you will knock your fucking socks off."

Leroy leaned forward. "I'm listening."

Annie picked up on the change in his demeanour. She mouthed, "What?"

He held up a hand as Mack started to speak. "You wouldn't believe what I came across. I need you to sit on most of what I'm about to tell you because I think I'm going to be busy. Anyhow, I found a file which was being compiled by an IA officer by the name of Ian Collier. He was killed in a car wreck a few years back. He had it hidden away because he didn't trust anyone. What it all comes down to is that Hoyland was on somebody's radar, Collier's."

"How?"

"Corruption is my guess. Links to the Italian Mafia. Anyhow, I found some photos in the file too. One was Guido Montanari, another was his accountant who disappeared, Dario Laterza, and I came across a picture of Tom Whitfield and his wife. For some reason Collier had a circle around her. You might want to do some background there."

"We've been doing a dive on Whitfield. His wife came up, but we never really looked at her. Now you've mentioned this, I'll go back over it."

"So, tell me, what do you have on Whitfield?"

"The guy who's good for the bombings was tied to him in Orange," Leroy explained. He then went on to tell Mack what else they'd found and the fact that Pietro had told Gloria about the real reason behind the bombing.

"Shit. Can you send me copies of what you have? I'll put a team together and see if I can work on something from this end."

"We should have confirmation on Hoyland soon. Nash had me give him some information to see if it would come back."

"How?"

Leroy told him.

"Fucking Nash. The bastard's crazy. He'll wind up dead one day."

"Let's hope it's not today. Gloria is on her way up there to see what the hell is happening. Can you give us anything?"

"I'll have another look through it and do what I can."

"Thanks."

Leroy hung up the phone and stared at Annie. She gave him an almost pleading look and asked, "Well?"

"Hang onto your hat, this just got more than a little interesting."

Leroy and Annie both looked into Whitfield's wife. It took them a while to track her history down because there was just nothing there. No trace whatsoever. It was like her past had been erased. All that was available was under the name of Arianna Whitfield.

They looked for a birth certificate, work history, Medicare, nothing. Then Annie looked into their wedding and struck silver. It wasn't gold because they would still have work to do, but it was a start.

"I've got something, Leroy," she sounded excited as she looked up from her laptop.

"What is it?"

"Our friends the Whitfields were married in Griffith."

"That is interesting. What are the odds she grew up there?"

Annie said, "It's possible. It's not really a place you would choose to get married if you didn't have family there or some other connection."

"Let's look at the school stuff again. We might just get lucky."

Annie looked at her watch. It was almost five. She reached for the phone. "Let's hope I get lucky."

"What are you doing?" Leroy asked, puzzled.

"I'm going to ring Griffith High School. You never know. I might come up with something."

Leroy nodded and gave a tired sigh. "It's worth a try, I guess."

Annie punched in the number listed on the school's website and listened to it ring. And ring. And ring.

Then it was picked up. "Griffith High School, Debbie speaking."

She sounded elderly.

"Debbie, this is Constable Annie Long from the Australian Federal Police. I was wondering if you might be able to help me?"

There was a long hesitation at the other end of the call before, "Ahh … sure, I hope so. What do you need?"

"This may be a long shot, but do you keep records of all of your past students?"

"Yes, we do. Who were you inquiring about?"

"We're not sure of her last name, but her first name would be Arianna."

"Oh, what a lovely name. Just give me a minute and I'll check on the computer. It's wonderful now, ever since we went electronic and transferred everything over.

There was a drawn-out silence and then Debbie said, "Oh dear, I didn't know we had that many."

"How many is that?"

"Seven."

Annie thought for a moment. "Let's say she was there ap-proximately twenty to twenty-five years ago."

"Mmm, that long. Give me a minute."

Silence again.

"There we go. I do love these computers. There was one Arianna here at that time."

"There was? Great. Could you tell me her last name?"

"Yes, dear. It was Montanari. Arianna Montanari."

"Holy shit!" Annie exclaimed.

"I beg your pardon?"

"I said thanks for your help, Debbie. You were marvellous."

"Thank you."

"No, thank you."

Annie hung up and stared at Leroy. "I was right. She did go to school there. Her name, her maiden name was Montanari. Arianna Montanari. Her father is the boss of the Italian Mafia."

CHAPTER THIRTY-SIX

Hoyland got out of his car and approached the black Bentley parked ahead of him in the alley. Two men climbed from it and met him halfway. The alley smelled like garbage and piss and any number of other things. He looked at the man in front of him and asked, "What was so important that we had to meet now?"

Tom Whitfield stared at him and then asked, "Where are you at with the investigation?"

"I've told my people to wind it up. They have their man and I've ordered Nash back from Collari. There should be no further issue out at Dawn Station from now on."

"Did you know that Gloria Browning went to speak to Agostino in Goulburn today?"

Hoyland frowned. "What? I had no idea. What about?"

"It doesn't take a genius to figure that out," Whitfield sneered. "Anyway, he has since met with an unfortunate accident."

"OK. Fine."

"Not fine. Your team is getting too close. We need to take action to make sure that they *do* back off."

"What do you have in mind?"

"Gloria Browning. Does she have any family?" Mario asked.

Hoyland stared at the dark-haired killer. "Why?"

"As Mr. Whitfield said, we need to make sure that they get the message."

"Wait a minute. I told you what was happening. There's no need to do whatever it is you're going to do."

"Are you going to answer the question, Pete?" Whitfield asked.

Hoyland was fully aware that Whitfield was a dangerous man, but right at that point in time, he was starting to understand just how dangerous, and wished he'd brought his gun with him instead of leaving it in the car. As far as he knew, Gloria only had Rachel and he wasn't about to give them a two-year-old.

"I – I can't," Hoyland stammered.

"I don't think you understand the predicament I'm in, Pete," Whitfield said to him. "In a very short time, days, in fact, I shall be the new prime minister of our great country. I'll not let all we've worked for be fucked up at the eleventh hour. Too much has been invested."

It suddenly dawned on Hoyland what was happening.

Whitfield was about to be prime minister and the Italian Mafia was about to become the most powerful criminal organization in the country.

And this meeting? It wasn't just about Gloria and her team. It was about tying up loose ends. And he was a thread they didn't care for. He tried to swallow and found his mouth dry. "I'm not going to give you what you want, Tom."

The pop of the silenced gun in Mario's hand signalled that the time for talk was over. Hoyland's right leg gave out beneath him and he collapsed in a heap with a sharp cry of pain. Whitfield's hired killer stepped forward, suddenly looking substantially larger than his six-feet. Pointing the gun at Hoyland, the killer said, "Let's try again, shall we?"

Mario shot Hoyland four times. The first three were what it took to find out about Gloria's daughter, Rachel, and the fact that Gloria wasn't home. Instead, she had a babysitter she relied upon. An ex-police woman named Pearl.

The last one was placed between his eyes to finish it.

Whitfield stood watching it all with indifference. When it was over, he said, "Get the kid tonight. She can be flown to Griffith. We'll keep her for as long as we need to."

"What about when we don't?" Mario asked, unscrewing the suppressor on his gun.

"Then she disappears."

CHAPTER THIRTY-SEVEN

An incessant banging on the door and ringing of the doorbell had Pearl well and truly pissed off by the time she opened it. The fact that some ignorant prick was doing it at this time of night and had woken the baby, did not help her mood one bit. She was that hellbent on giving the bastard a piece of her mind that she never once thought about all that was going on in Gloria's life at that point.

She opened the door and saw a man standing there, his hand holding a suppressed gun that was pointed right at her. Shock registered on her face as it coughed, and a red blossom appeared on her chest. She staggered back and he shot her again. This time, Pearl fell to the floor of the hallway.

Mario stepped over her and closed the door. Then he followed the sound of Rachel's distressed cries all the way to her bedroom.

COLLARI
TUESDAY, 3:00 AM

"Shit!" Gloria exclaimed as she swung hard on the wheel of her unmarked Commodore to get around a pothole that looked more like a moon crater in the middle of the street. The car swung violently before she regained control and straightened it again.

Fatigue was in every muscle. Since darkness had fallen, it had taken all her concentration to dodge the holes in the road, kangaroos, cows, and even a damned wild pig. The constant staring made her eyes feel like they were full of gravel.

Gloria swung the car onto the narrow main street. It was dark except for a single light outside the hotel, and the only vehicle she saw, was parked across the road from it. When she drew level, she indicated and swung into a carpark outside the front door.

Killing the lights, she cut the engine, then sat there for a moment looking at the chalkboard sign on the wall beside the door. It was telling her she could get sausages and chips and a beer for nine-fifty on Tuesdays. "Sounds good," she muttered.

Sitting there, Gloria contemplated climbing out of the car and bashing on the door. "Fuck it," she growled and started the car again. Backing out of the park, she went looking for the police station.

She found it within two minutes, and there was a light on inside. A duty officer, she guessed, was in there probably bored out of his brain. Once again, Gloria turned the car off and this time she climbed out and approached the front door and tried it. Locked.

Pounding on the door briefly, she then stood and waited. About two minutes later a tired-looking constable opened the door. "Yeah, what?"

Gloria flashed her badge and immediately his attitude changed. "I'm Sergeant Gloria Browning, AFP. I believe you have one of mine in your lockup. I'm here to collect him."

"I can't just let him out, ma'am. Not without telling my sergeant."

"That's exactly what you're going to do unless you want me to ring command in Sydney. Wake someone up and see how they like it."

The constable paled. "I guess I can let him out, ma'am."

"Good, let's go, shall we?"

She followed him into the office, then out to the cells, and he opened the one Nash was in. When the door swung open, the PI was standing there ready to take on whatever came through the door at that ungodly hour. Instead, he saw Gloria. "It's kick-out time, Nash, let's go."

"You're a sight for sore eyes, Gloria."

"Don't get all happy and shit," she growled. "I'm tired, cranky, and damned hungry."

Nash stared at the constable. "Where's my Glock?"

"In the gun safe."

"Get it. Along with the rest of my stuff."

"Yes, sir."

Five minutes later they were standing outside. Nash said,

"Thanks for coming to get me out."

"Get you out?" she snapped. "After the stupid fucking stunt you pulled, I should have left your arse there!"

"It worked, though."

"We'll talk about that in the morning. Or when the sun comes up. Some bullshit like that. I've just driven over twelve hours and my brain is fried. Can you get into the hotel?"

"Yes."

"Good. Looks like your bed is it. And if you touch me, I'll cut your dick off."

"Wouldn't dream of it."

CHAPTER THIRTY-EIGHT

COLLARI
4:30 AM

It wasn't Nash that Gloria had to worry about. It was herself. And once their wild throes of passion had abated, they both lay there staring into the darkness above them.

"That was unexpected," Nash said.

"Shut up."

"Hey, I'm not complaining."

"Just leave it."

"OK."

Silence ensued once more. Then, "What did you find out?" Gloria asked Nash.

"I found where they pump the water underground into the aquifer. And I also found out that Hoyland is definitely bent. But the biggest thing I learned yesterday was that Dario Laterza is still alive and kicking and living out at Dawn Station."

"Dario Laterza, the Mafia accountant?"

"The one and only. I figure he's running the operation out there."

"Bloody hell."

"Exactly. Now, what do you have?"

Gloria filled him in on what she'd learned. From the visit in prison to the phone call, she'd received from Annie the previous evening about Whitfield. Nash chuckled.

"What's so funny?" Gloria asked him.

"Whitfield's married to the mob and about to become prime minister of our country. This didn't just happen. It was a well-orchestrated plan."

"And now that things are starting to go sideways, they'll be looking to tidy up loose ends before they derail everything," Gloria surmised.

Nash said, "That would be my guess. I'd say that's why Pietro was killed, and why Hoyland has ordered me back. Can't have the golden child tied to the theft of water or the Mafia."

"It would also be why Hoyland ordered me to shut down the investigation," Gloria said. "We have our bomber and there is to be no further investigation. Just like Orange."

"The question is, where do we go next?"

"I guess we wait and see what Mack has in that file."

"Mmm, that will be interesting. This Collier must have been onto something."

Gloria yawned. "I'm tired. I'm going to sleep. We'll talk more later."

Nash ran a hand up her bare thigh. Gloria said, "Sleep, Nash."

CANBERRA
8:03 AM

Annie slammed down the phone and rushed from her office. After such a late night, the last thing she felt like doing was rolling on a murder. Not really their thing, only this one was different. She hurried along to Leroy's office and walked in. He looked up and saw the expression on her face and said, "What?"

"Someone has killed Hoyland."

There was no slowing down or stopping until they reached the crime scene. Cops were everywhere. After all, Hoyland was one of their own. Leroy and Annie climbed from their car and walked to where the body lay. It was covered and Leroy reached down and pulled the sheet back.

"Fucking bastards," a cop said from behind them.

Leroy covered the body again and he and Annie turned to face the speaker.

The cop said, "Fucking tortured him. Why else would they shoot him so many times like that?"

Annie and Leroy stared at one another and after a moment, Leroy motioned her to one side. He said, "What do you think?"

"I think whoever did this was after something."

"Yeah. Or to silence him."

"Fuck it, ring Gloria."

COLLARI
8:45 AM

Nash bit Gloria's neck as her fingernails raked down his back, drawing deep red lines which would rise into welts. They'd slept until eight-thirty and upon waking, one thing had led to another and here they were, going for it once more.

Then the phone rang. "Christ!" Gloria hissed.

"Don't answer it," Nash growled, not wanting to lose their rhythm.

"I have to, it could be Pearl."

"Who's Pearl?"

"My babysitter."

"Oh, OK," Nash sighed and rolled to the side.

After fumbling with the mobile, Gloria managed to hit answer and get it to her ear. "Hello?"

"We have your daughter. Back off the investigation."

"What? Who is this?"

The line went dead.

"Oh, God, no."

Nash sat up. "What's wrong."

"They said they have Rachel."

"Who?"

"I don't know."

"What else did they say?"

"Nothing."

"Gloria, think."

"To back off the investigation," she snapped. "I have to ring

Pearl."

"Do you think she'll answer?"

"I don't fucking know!" she shrieked. *"They have my little girl!"*

"Give me your phone."

Gloria passed it over and buried her face in her hands. Nash punched in a number and Annie answered. "I was just about to call you. There's some bad shit gone down here last night."

"Annie, just wait. I need you to go around to Gloria's and check on Rachel."

"Why, what's happened?"

"Now, Annie. Take Leroy with you. Call me back when you get there."

"Sure. But before you go, you should know that someone shot Hoyland last night. It looks like they tortured him for some reason before they put the kill shot into him."

She hung up and Nash glanced at Gloria. *I think I know why.* "Gloria?"

She looked up at him, tears streaming down her cheeks. "What?"

"Someone killed Hoyland last night. Annie said he took a while to die. Like they were trying to get something out of him."

Several emotions crossed her face at once upon hearing the news. The last one was a questioning stare at Nash. "You think that it was about Rachel?"

"Yes. That plus tying up loose ends."

"We have to get her back, Nash. She's only a baby. She's all I have."

"We'll get her back, OK? That's if they have her. In the meantime, we have to work out what they want and where they've taken her."

"I told you. They want us to back off the investigation."

"All right. So, if they have her, it will be Whitfield or the Italians."

Gloria stared hard at him. "How can you be so calm?"

"I'm not calm, Gloria. I'm just trying to focus on getting your little girl back."

"Ours, Dave," Gloria said in a soft voice. "Our little girl."

Even though he'd suspected what had just been confirmed, it still came like a kick in the guts. He opened his mouth to speak but nothing came out. Instead, he reached out and took Gloria in his arms and held her.

CHAPTER THIRTY-NINE

Their car came to a halt in the driveway and the doors flew open. Leroy and Annie came out of the car and drew their weapons. They approached the front door in silence and before they got there, Leroy gave Annie a signal to tell her to head around the back.

Once on the doorstep, Leroy gave her thirty more seconds to get into position and he tried the door. It was open. Swinging it open, the first thing he saw was the large strip of blood on the floor headed along the hallway.

Leroy brought his sidearm up and stepped inside. As he went through the house, he cleared each room before meeting up with Annie in the kitchen. She was bending over the still form of Pearl, checking for any sign of life. Looking up, she said, "She's alive. Must've been trying to reach a phone."

Leroy took his mobile from his pocket and dialled 000. As he waited for an answer he said, "The baby's gone."

COLLARI
9:20 AM

"The baby's gone, Nash," Annie said in a soft voice. "Pearl is down. She was shot but she's hanging in there."

He looked across the room at Gloria. Speaking softly to Annie, he said, "Listen, Gloria got a call a while back saying that Rachel had been taken and we're to back off the investigation."

"It has to be Whitfield."

"That's what we were thinking."

"What do you want us to do?"

"Keep working it from your end. Not the Whitfield thing, but the kidnapping and Pearl's shooting. I've had a thought about what to do. Just keep at it and wait for one of us to call."

"What are you going to do?"

Nash said one word. "Katanka."

CANBERRA
9:23 AM

"That's all he said?" Leroy asked. "Katanka? What the fuck does that mean?"

"I think it means he's going off the reservation," Annie proposed. "He just didn't want to say anything."

Leroy shook his head. He wanted to do something to help. Instead … "OK. Take the car, Annie and put us together some go bags and stash them in the boot. Put in weapons, ammunition, vests, and anything else you think we might need."

"What are you thinking?"

First, I'm going to hand this off to someone else, and then we're going on a little road trip."

"What? Where?"

"We know this is linked to Whitfield, right?"

"Right."

"He's not going to want to have Rachel anywhere near him just in case this goes south on him. So, where's the best place to hide her?"

Annie stared at him for a moment, her mind ticking over. Then it came to her. "Griffith."

"Yeah. That's what I reckon. If it's so, then that's where Gloria and Nash will eventually land. When they do, I want to be there to help."

COLLARI
9:31 AM

"I have a plan to get Rachel back," Nash told Gloria.

She looked at him with red-rimmed eyes. "What?"

"We need something that they want."

"Really?" the sarcasm dripped from every word. "Who are you? Fucking Einstein?"

Nash let it go. "They sell all of the water they steal, but to keep track of it, they must have some kind of ledger. I'm thinking that is what Laterza is for. He's there overseeing the operation and fudging the books."

"Even if it's true, how do you intend to get it?"

"By going out to Dawn Station and stealing it."

"You're crazy," Gloria told him. "There are rules, procedures which have to be followed."

"Not for me. Technically I'm not a cop anymore. All I care about is getting Rachel back."

Gloria stood up. "I'm coming with you. Someone has to watch your back."

"All right, but first I need to get to my Landcruiser. It has everything I need in it."

Gloria drove him down to the boat ramp carpark where he'd left the vehicle the day before. It was still there, and it all looked fine. Except for the slashed tires and the dinghy. It looked as though when Jacko had brought it back, he'd taken the plug out, and it was now almost completely submerged in the murky brown water. "Someone's being childish."

Nash opened the back of the vehicle and unlocked the lock-box, removing his vest, ammunition, magazines, and lastly the M4 carbine. He was about to put it in the back of Gloria's car when the sound of an engine reached his ears. Looking up, he cursed when he saw the police car pulling into the carpark.

Royall came to a crunching halt on a gravel-filled pothole and opened his door. Climbing out, the police sergeant looked anything but happy. "Just what the hell do you think you're doing?"

Nash put the carbine in the Commodore and shut the door. He stared at Royall and said, "Going to make an arrest."

It was a lie, but Royall didn't know that.

"Where?" he demanded. "And why wasn't I told? You were ordered back to Canberra by your boss."

His gaze flicked across to Gloria. "And who the hell are you?"

"I'm his boss. Sergeant Gloria Browning."

Nash said, "Come on, Gloria, let's go."

"Wait," Royall snapped and dug into his pocket for a phone. "I'm ringing Hoyland. He'll sort you both out."

"Hoyland's dead," Nash told him. "He was executed last night."

That stopped Royall in his tracks. He gave Nash a funny look and shook his head. "No, I don't believe you."

Gloria said, "Believe it. Whoever killed him did so for information so they could kidnap my daughter."

The police sergeant went quiet.

"Face it, Royall. Whitfield is tying up loose ends. Right about now I'd say you're wondering if you are next. And I'd say that it's a good possibility."

"Who are you arresting?"

"Laterza."

"You're going out to Dawn Station?"

"How familiar are you with things out there, Royall?" Nash asked.

"Why?"

"I take it that you know they steal water and hide it in an aquifer," Nash said. "Quite confident in fact. I also think you know what happened to Ray Petersen. Am I right?"

"No. I've no idea."

They could tell he was lying. "Come on, Royall. The only way to save yourself is to come clean. Maybe you might be able to get a deal if you testify."

The police sergeant thought about his answer. Then he said, "All right. But I'm not saying a word until I see a deal."

"Wrong, Royall," Nash said. "I want to know if Laterza has some kind of ledger out at Dawn Station which he keeps a tally of the water in?"

"I'm not saying anything. Not without a deal."

Gloria moved with lightning speed. Her Glock was out in a flash and she'd closed the distance between them in an instant. The handgun was jammed up under his chin and she hissed, "Listen here, motherfucker. The pricks have my daughter. We figure we can make a trade for her. Now, do they have a ledger or not? Think carefully before answering because you only get one shot at this."

Royall nodded jerkily. "Laterza has one so they can keep track of the water."

"For who?"

"Whitfield. It was his planning, but Montanari was the

money behind it. That's why Laterza is here. He was about to be pounced on by organized crime, so they made him disappear."

"Who killed Ray Petersen?"

"Ringa."

Gloria lowered the Glock and pushed him away from her. "Go home. You're done."

"Wait. Who killed Reilly?" Nash asked.

"Ringa."

"Right. Get. And if you think about warning them out at Dawn Station, think again. Because I'll come back here and put a bullet in your brain myself."

They watched him go and Nash turned to Gloria. "Not too late to rethink."

"I'm going, Nash."

"Fine. Let's go."

CHAPTER FORTY

From the main gate to the homestead, the distance was approximately two kilometres. Nash and Gloria hid the car in the scrub about a hundred meters down the gravel road. It was also sufficiently far enough away from the CCTV camera stationed to observe the comings and goings, to be out of view.

They put on their tactical vests and loaded them up with magazines. Lastly, they checked their M4s to make sure they were sound. A murder of crows started their noisy cawing in a large Rivergum at the edge of the paddock. Nash gave a wry smile and wondered if they knew more than he did.

"Are you ready?" he asked Gloria.

She nodded.

"Nervous?" Nash said as he slapped a box magazine home into his weapon.

"Why would I be nervous? I'm with a crazy prick like you. What could go wrong?"

He smiled at her sarcasm and she saw the same look in his eyes she'd seen that time in Katanka. It sent a shiver down her spine.

"We'll circle around to our left and keep to the trees at the edge of the paddock for as long as we can. Then we'll be out in the open I'm afraid."

Gloria said, "Let's go, Gunga Din."

They made it into the Rivergums without any problems. From there they pressed forward, keeping the thick trunks between themselves and their target. The trees showed the scars of many floods over the years. Watermarks in some parts, while others still had tell-tale debris wedged in their forks. One had a rusted water tank stuck some ten-feet up it in a junction.

In a couple of places, deep washes had been scoured out by fast-flowing water. They used these to their advantage by jumping down into them and making further progress below line of sight.

That was fine, but when they were still a thousand meters out, they ran out of cover. Nash dropped to a knee and Gloria did the same behind him. A fly buzzed around his head and he swiped it away. A thin bead of sweat trickled down the side of his face.

"This is where it gets tricky," he said to Gloria. "I'll start across, and then you give me one minute before you move."

"Don't you want me with you?"

"We keep spread out. That way if I come under fire, there will be less risk of us both getting hit at the same time."

Gloria didn't like it, but it made sense. "OK. Just remember to duck."

Nash started forward out of the trees, the flies seeming to get thicker as he did. His boots crunched on the dry soil of the plowed paddock and every now and then he kicked a clod. The deep furrows in the earth slowed him down, and his M4 was up at his shoulder, ready should he need to shoot in a hurry. And suddenly Nash felt something he hadn't felt in a long while. Alive!

As he drew closer to the homestead, things seemed to take shape before him. Windows, the veranda, water tanks, a fence, gardens ... he stopped and dropped to a knee - then waved Gloria forward.

"What's up?"

"It's too quiet. I've not seen any movement at all."

Gloria studied the structures before them. "Do you think they know?"

"I'm not sure. Come on. Make for the stockyards. From there we can circle around the machinery shed and then to the back of the house."

Nash started forward again, the sun beating down on his exposed skin. Reaching the stockyards, he climbed through steel rails, then crossed the dry yard to the other side. Resting the barrel of the carbine on a rail, he waited for Gloria to join him.

The next challenge was to get to the huge machinery shed. Nash slipped through the opening between the yard rails once more and scooted across to the corrugated steel structure. He slipped inside and once more waited for Gloria.

She appeared at his side and looked around. A John Deere tractor and harvester were parked side-by-side. On the far side of those was what looked to be a large herbicide spray kit that got towed behind the tractor. Beside it was a flatbed truck.

Nash moved to a position near the harvester that gave him a better view of the house. He stood and peered around the front of the machine, looking for any sign of life. Still nothing. About to take a step forward, he halted when Gloria grasped his shoulder. Turning to look at her, he saw that she had turned deathly pale. "What?"

She pointed to the dusty earth of the shed floor. Nash looked down and saw the reason for her angst.

A snake. Not just any snake. At least six-feet of one of the deadliest serpents in the world. An Eastern Brown. Nash froze. The reptile paused, flicking the air with its tongue, and then moved off under the harvester. He breathed a sigh of relief and looked at Gloria.

She mouthed "What the fuck?"

He shrugged, just glad the damned thing had moved on without any fuss. Once again, he was about to make towards the house when he was interrupted. This time by the sound of approaching vehicles closing at speed.

Both he and Gloria ducked back behind the harvester and waited. There were two four-wheel drives. They stopped near the machinery shed and six men got out then rushed into the house. As they went, Nash heard Laterza call out to Ringa, "Are you sure the sensors are working properly? They weren't yesterday."

"They're fucking fine. I fixed them."

"Sensors?" Gloria asked.

"They've got everything else."

"What do we do now?"

Nash thought for a moment and got that crazy look in his eyes again. "Follow me."

"What the fuck?" Gloria blurted out as he began walking toward the house.

CHAPTER FORTY-ONE

As Nash passed through the open door, he met one of the hands coming back the other way. Reversing the M4, he brought its butt sharply forward just as the man started to say, "What th –"

Collapsing like a poleaxed steer, the hand made no further sound. Nash brought the carbine back up to his shoulder and kept moving. The short rear entryway opened out into the kitchen. Another man was standing at the counter, looking at something. He glanced up and saw Nash with the M4 pointed at him and his jaw dropped.

The PI lifted a finger to his lips, indicating for him to be quiet, then walked around the counter to the stunned man and whispered, "Where are the rest?"

Pointing to a hallway, the man said, "Down there in the

office where the CCTVs are."

"Thanks," Nash said and hit him a savage blow that dropped him like his friend.

There was movement and Nash glanced up to see Gloria standing there, a stunned expression on her face. He pointed to the hallway and moved in that direction. It opened out into a large living area with leather lounge, piano, large flat screen tv, double sliding glass doors, a wood fire, and a bookshelf that encompassed the whole of one wall. Things had flowed smoothly so far, but everything changed in the next heartbeat.

A third man appeared from a room located at the left of the living room, catching Nash by surprise. His hand dove for the handgun tucked into his waistband, and he almost had it out before Nash blew off two shots which knocked him back.

A flurry of curses erupted from the room down the hall and then another of Ringa's thugs appeared with a pump-action shotgun. Obviously, one that had missed the buy-back scheme. He fired once and the air filled with small deadly pellets.

Nash dived for cover behind the lounge just as the man fired, and the shot flew overhead, blowing a hole in the wall to the right of where Gloria stood. She reacted instantly and sprayed the area with 5.56 rounds. Holes opened in the wall, and the shooter jerked under each bullet impact. Red began to show on his cotton shirt where holes had appeared, and he fell to the floor, dead.

Gloria then took cover behind a recliner chair, aware that it was not going to stop a bullet if they shot at her. Jacko and Ringa appeared from the hallway, Jacko holding a handgun, while the ex-SAS man had his own carbine. Ringa let rip with a long burst and the bullets punched into the lounge, walls, and chair. Gloria and Nash got as low as they could to create the smallest possible targets. Small ornaments on a shelf attached to the wall behind them shattered under the weight of gunfire.

Jacko joined the party and started to rattle off his own fire with methodical ease.

"Changing!" Nash heard Ringa cry out as his magazine went dry. It was all the invitation Nash needed and he rose. The sights settled on Ringa who was fumbling with a magazine, arrogantly standing out in the open. The PI stroked the trigger on his M4 twice and the rounds hammered into Ringa's torso.

The killer's jaw dropped as he sank to his knees, the magazine falling from his grasp. With his strength waning, Ringa's carbine succumbed to the forces of gravity.

"This is for Petersen, you prick," Nash muttered and shot him in the face.

Behind the chair, Gloria flipped her fire selector around to semi and eased herself level with the leather arm to aim at Jacko. Seeing her break cover, he fired two shots in her direction. Both punched through the back of the chair, missing her by a narrow margin. Gloria fired and didn't miss.

Jacko cried out as one bullet ripped into him low in the torso, while the other tore flesh at his throat. The slug severed the carotid artery and blood sprayed up the wall and across the floor. Slumping onto his side, he began to bleed out, making a ghastly gurgling sound and spasming violently.

That left only one. Laterza.

"Are you there, Dario?" Nash called out.

"I'm here."

"Time to come out. The others won't be any help to you now. Are you armed?"

There was a thud as the Mafia accountant threw his handgun out onto the floor. "Now it's your turn," Nash snapped.

Walking nervously through the open doorway, his eyes rolling wildly in his head, Laterza was trying to comprehend what had just happened.

"Sit on the lounge."

Gloria walked over to him and stared hard into his face. "Where's your ledger?"

"My what?"

Gloria lowered the barrel of her M4 and pushed it against his upper thigh. When she spoke, her voice was low and clear, enunciating each syllable with more than a hint of menace so there could be no misinterpretation. "Listen here, motherfucker. Whitfield has my daughter so I'm in no mood for your bullshit. This is a one-time deal. You speak or I'll fucking shoot you. And don't try any of your *omertà* bullshit either. I'm not in the fucking mood."

Laterza glanced at Nash who smiled coldly at the accountant. "Don't look at me, arsehole. She'll do it and I'll let her. The girl is my daughter too."

For a moment Laterza thought Gloria wasn't serious. But something about the look in her eyes told him otherwise. He pointed towards the room containing the CCTVs where he and the others had been checking the footage. "It is in there. On a shelf that has books on it. It is hidden behind them. A red ledger."

Nash hurried down the hall and entered the room. Looking about, he saw a desk in the centre of the room and three monitors on the wall. Each of them were steadily scrolling through different CCTV camera feeds. There was other electrical equipment there too. But Nash wasn't interested in any of that. He walked to the shelf with the books on it and dug around until he found what he was looking for. Opening the ledger, he flicked through page after page of entries. Smiling, he walked back to join the others in the living area. "Got it."

Gloria nodded and said to Laterza, "Give me your phone."

The accountant reached into his pocket and withdrew it. He passed it to Gloria who scrolled through his list of contacts, looking for the name she wanted. It wasn't there. "What's Montanari's number?"

He remained mute so Gloria raised the M4's barrel and pointed it at his face. "Number?"

"It is under the name F. Farmer."

Gloria raised her eyebrows. "As in fruit farmer?"

"Yes."

Nash said, "Before you do this, Gloria, remember what we discussed on the way out here. Make sure the old prick understands it."

"I will," she said and called the number that came up under F. Farmer. She waited for it to be answered and then said, "I have your ledger. If you want it, we need to meet."

She listened for a minute or so and then said, "We'll bring it to you. But first, there are a couple of conditions."

CHAPTER FORTY-TWO

MONTANARI FARMS, GRIFFITH
WEDNESDAY, 1:00 PM

The unmarked Commodore eased to a stop at the main entrance gate to Montanari Farms and Nash and Gloria climbed out. There waiting for them were Leroy and Annie. Both were kitted out as though going on a raid; vests on and armed to the teeth.

"What are you two doing out here, anyway?" Gloria asked. She'd called them the day before and found out what they were up to, grateful for their initiative and backup.

"Two and two make four," Leroy said. "We figured Whitfield wouldn't want to have Rachel in close proximity to him. This seemed like the most logical place to hide her."

In the distance, the steady beat of a helicopter rotor grew louder. They all turned to stare to the east. The Bell 429 Global Ranger in the distance grew gradually bigger until it was overhead, and the sound was almost deafening.

They watched it circle and put down near the house. Nash turned to Gloria. "This is it."

She frowned. "What do you mean?"

"This is as far as you go."

"Bullshit!" she almost exploded. "I'm coming with you."

"No. I'll get Rachel and bring her to you. Listen, it will be better all-round if you don't come. You'd be a federal cop trading evidence with a bad guy for the safe return of your daughter. Besides, I have a plan which will allow us to get our man, kind of. I'll take our friend and the ledger. If it all goes wrong, you lot come in and save the day."

Gloria was set to argue some more, but Nash cut her off by saying, "I've got this, Gloria. Let me save her for you. I've not been around to do much else."

"You'd better not fuck this up, Nash," Gloria said, tears starting to fill her eyes. "Or I'll shoot you myself."

Nash climbed back into the Commodore and started it up. He selected drive and eased off the brake. The Commodore moved forward and as it did, he wondered whether he could deliver without getting himself killed.

When Nash stopped the Commodore and climbed out, he was met by two of Guido Montanari's bodyguards. Together they helped Laterza from the back seat and then frisked the PI for a weapon.

When they found the Glock, one of them stared at Nash

who shrugged and said, "I'll have that back when we're done."

The second of the bodyguards reached out and went to relieve him of the ledger but Nash stayed his hand. "No, my friend, this isn't for you. You touch it and I'll break your arm."

The man smiled and nodded. "OK. Follow me."

They took him inside where he found everyone gathered in the large living room. Montanari, Whitfield, Mario, and now the two bodyguards, himself, and Laterza. Montanari studied him and asked, "Where is the woman I spoke with?"

"Not far away. I'm Nash."

He nodded his recognition and pointed at the ledger. "You will give me that now."

Nash chuckled. "The fuck I will. Where's the child?"

Montanari nodded to one of his bodyguards who subsequently left the room. "She will be here soon."

"What happened at Dawn Station?" Whitfield snapped.

Nash said coolly, "You'll need some new workers."

"Son of a bitch," he hissed. "Do you really think you'll leave here alive?"

Nash's face grew hard and he hissed, "How anyone would vote for a person like you has got me fucked."

He was set to continue, but Arianna appeared holding the baby, accompanied by the bodyguard. She handed Rachel over to Nash and then left the room. He looked her over perfunctorily and she seemed fine, smelled clean even like she'd just had a bath.

"The book," Montanari said.

Nash handed it over.

"Mario," Whitfield snapped. "Kill him."

"Wait!" Montanari shouted. "I want to hear what else he has to say. What he knows."

Nash nodded. "OK. Let's start with your boy there. To put it bluntly, he's fucked. We can link him to the bombing of the senator as well as the one in Orange. I think we might be able to link his boy Mario to Goulburn as well. Depends on whether he threw away the gun that he used to shoot Flaherty with. Also, Pietro sang like a canary, I'm told, and we have him giving a statement about how Whitfield was behind the bombing and coerced him into taking the fall."

Nash left out the part where Pietro had implicated Montanari as well. "Also, we should be able to link him to the death of Peter Hoyland. Then we can throw in the testimony of one Chris Royall, who should be able to pin something else on him, and I'd say yeah, he's fucked."

"Kill him and be done with it, Guido," Whitfield snapped. "I need to get back to Canberra for the ballot tomorrow."

"So, it's on for tomorrow, is it?" Nash asked sarcastically.

"Yes. Not that you'll be around to see it."

Nash ignored him and said, "Thing is, Guido. You and I both know Whitfield is screwed. Once they get him in the lockup, they'll question the crap out of him. How many years do you figure he'll get? Twenty? Forty? Either way, once that key turns, he'll be looking to make a deal. And who do you think he's going to turn on?"

"What? No!" Whitfield blurted out. He could see what Nash was trying to do and it scared the hell out of him.

Nash continued. "All I want to do is to take Rachel out of here and you'll never see me again. As for Whitfield, I'll leave him here with you. Let you figure out what to do with him. Or …"

He left it to hang and could see Montanari was giving it serious consideration. "The alternative is that you can kill me now and there'll be three federal cops with automatic weapons climbing up your arse in minutes. Up to you. All I want to do is go home, back to being a PI."

"And I will never see you again?"

"Never."

There was a long silence before Montanari said, "OK. Go. Take the child. I am not a kidnapper of children. If I want something done to someone, I have them killed."

Nash felt the tension evaporate from his body. "Thank you."

As he started towards the door, he heard Whitfield say, "You can't let him go, Guido. He'll ruin everything."

"It is you who have ruined everything, you idiot."

Nash heard no more for he was out the door. He sat Rachel on the front seat and drove slowly towards the gate where Gloria and the others waited for him.

CHAPTER FORTY-THREE

" *... Police are no closer to discovering the whereabouts of Water Minister Thomas Whitfield who has been missing now for two weeks. He was once touted to be the next prime minister ...*"

Nash turned the television off and picked up the small doll that Rachel had just dropped. Gloria entered the living room and said, "I was talking to Mack earlier today. He's slowly putting things together with the help of Royall."

"How's yours going?"

"Good, that ledger helped out no end."

On the way to Griffith, they had stopped and photocopied the whole book for later reference. Nash would keep his word and never go back to Griffith again, but the AFP were all over Montanari's arse like fleas. The Mafia man was being investigated for his part in the water scam and the murder of New

South Wales Police Officer Ian Collier.

Eventually, they would get him for the murder of Whitfield and his man Mario, along with the accountant Laterza. His daughter Arianna was sent back to Italy.

"What do you suppose happened to Whitfield?" Gloria asked.

Nash ran his hand through Rachel's hair. Looking up at him, the little girl smiled. He said, "I don't know. He'll turn up one day. How's Pearl?"

"Great. She'll be back on her feet in no time."

"Good."

"With Ringa dead they still haven't been able to find Ray Petersen yet."

"Maybe they will, maybe they won't."

"What about you?" Gloria asked. "Are we going to see more of you?"

He poked Rachel on the tip of her nose, making her giggle. "Just try keeping me away."

Nash had been right. Whitfield did turn up. Bits of him anyway. Two months later, police found a number of fingers and toes amongst the fruit trees on Montanari farms, decayed, but DNA is a wonderful thing. They were able to identify three different men from their initial find; Whitfield, Mario, and Laterza. A secondary sweep uncovered no less than nine further victims of Montanari's infamous chipper.

He was indicted on twenty-seven charges including thirteen counts of murder, Ian Collier being one of them. He was sentenced to thirteen life sentences and change. Throughout the whole ordeal, Montanari kept alive the Mafia code of *Omertà.*

ABOUT THE AUTHORS

A relative newcomer to the world of writing, Brent Towns self-published his first book, a western, in 2015. Last Stand in Sanctuary took him two years to write. His first hardcover book, a Black Horse Western, was published the following year. Since then, he has written a further 26 western stories, including some in collaboration with British western author, Ben Bridges.

A country town in Queensland, Australia, is where Brent lives with his wife, Sam and son.

Sam Towns is a mother of one, toiler of many words, and spends most of her time fixing Brent's mistakes.

A LOOK AT: RETRIBUTION: A TEAM REAPER THRILLER

After he is betrayed and shoots the two most powerful men in the Irish Mob, John "Reaper" Kane is forced into hiding. He thinks Retribution, Arizona, is the perfect hiding place, but he is wrong. Underneath the old, crusty surface of the dying town, hides the Montoya Cartel, for they use it as a funnel to ship their drugs across the border.

Trying to lay low in a town gripped with lawlessness is impossible for the ex-recon marine, especially after the local sheriff is brutally murdered by the Montoya Cartel's sicario, leaving an old friend, Deputy Sheriff Cara Billings, the only person standing between them and the town.

Things go from bad to worse when Kane is arrested by Cleaver, the deputy in the cartel's pocket, for shooting a local gang member.

Enter DEA Agent Luis Ferrero who has expressed to his bosses for a long time the need for a task force to fight the cartels on their own ground. He's about to get his wish, and to head up his team, he wants the Reaper.

A thrill ride that doesn't let you go – Retribution is the first novel in the action-packed Reaper Series.

AVAILABLE NOW